"This is Craig Fellowes speaking," the horrid voice said.

Edwina tried to speak, but the effort came out a croak. "Is my husband all right?"

"Come now, Miss Crusoe, don't be nervous with me." Fellowes sounded amused and pleased. "Just don't lie to me, and everything will turn out just fine. Lying is a sin, you know, and besides, I can tell. I can tell when people are lying to me."

His voice hardened on the words. From behind them came a faint metallic creaking that Edwina found familiar but could not place.

"Why are you calling me, Mr. Fellowes?"

"I'm calling you for the same reason everyone calls you," Craig Fellowes said. "I want you to find me a murderer. Listen carefully, now. I'm only going to say this once. I know who killed the doctor, his secretary and the other one. You find out, bring the killer to me. You do that and I'll trade with you, mine for yours."

Edwina gripped the receiver with both hands. "Fine. Only not if you hurt him. If he's hurt or harmed in any way—"

"I'll decide," Craig Fellowes whispered, "who gets hurt." His voice went abruptly cold. "If anyone tries to stop me," he warned, "I'll be very angry. So wait for my next call and be ready, and don't screw up. Now that we're such good friends—"

He laughed a high, hideous sound, "I would hate to have to punish you . . ."

CADAVER

MARY KITTREDGE

ST. MARTIN'S PAPERBACKS

CADAVER

Copyright © 1992 by Mary Kittredge.

Cover illustration by Cameron Wasson.

All rights reserved. No part of this book may be used or reproduced in any manner whatsoever without written permission except in the case of brief quotations embodied in critical articles or reviews. For information address St. Martin's Press, 175 Fifth Avenue, New York, N.Y. 10010.

Library of Congress Catalog Card Number: 91-40329

ISBN: 0-312-95002-0

Printed in the United States of America

St. Martin's Press hardcover edition/April 1992
St. Martin's Paperbacks edition/June 1993

10 9 8 7 6 5 4 3 2

ONE

I CAN'T, thought licensed practical nurse Cleta Bell of the task immediately confronting her. But she had no choice, and as if recognizing this, her body continued lumbering down the dimly lit hospital corridor toward the dark open doorway of room 314. It was a private room, her final stop on 2:00 A.M. rounds; all she had to do was enter it, measure the blood pressure and temperature of the patient within, and take his pulse.

That she was to perform these tasks on a patient locked in leather restraints posed, to Cleta, no particular obstacle. That she had been advised on no account to let her hands stray near the patient's teeth was likewise of small concern. In her twenty years of nursing, she had learned to deal with kickers, punchers, pinchers, biters, spitters, feelers, and excretors of the most astonishing—although not, anymore, to Cleta—variety.

What she hadn't learned to deal with was murderers, but one was waiting for her now in room 314 and by all accounts he was a pip.

The cop in the chair outside the room looked up. Not much more than a kid, the cop had curly brown hair, a square solid jaw, and the winning smile of a fellow who had not yet met his match.

We'll see, Cleta thought grimly. From inside the room came the sounds of even snoring, the steady beeping of the cardiac monitor, and the sweet, pungent reek of paraldehyde. Toxic and old-fashioned, as a sedative the stuff still delivered a solid lights-out punch to even the most disruptive chronic boozer.

Which—among other things—this patient was. Mentally Cleta congratulated the ER resident nervy enough to prescribe a good stiff dose. Meanwhile she was also aware that the snoring had begun only as she drew within earshot.

And this, she knew instantly, was wrong. Cleta was big, but she was silent; no one ever heard her coming. On top of that was the matter of resisting the paraldehyde, another thing that until now she would not have thought possible.

"Time to check on our boy?" the young cop asked. Getting up, he shifted pleasurably under the official weight of his uniform, his badge and handcuffs, his wide black belt with its bright row of bullets and the holster at his hip.

Seeing what a novelty it all still was to him, Cleta felt not at all comforted by his presence as she took the clipboard from the rack outside the patient's room and pretended to examine it.

"You want to be careful in there," the young

cop said with a heavy frown of authority. "This guy's a real comedian."

Replacing the clipboard, she gave the young cop the briefest of flat stares. From inside the room the snoring sounds continued, too measured and deliberate now to be anything but feigned.

A comedian, Cleta thought, recalling the report she had received with her assignment. Upon his arrival in the emergency room, the patient had been noted to be a young white male, appearing unkempt, combative, and disoriented, and suffering from injuries and ailments including but not limited to:

(1) Superficial gunshot wound to the forearm; cleansed, stitched, and dressed, consult to plastics initiated

(2) Moderate to severe chronic malnutrition; consult to dietary sent

(3) Numerous partially healed deep puncture wounds to the hands and feet, possibly self-inflicted; consults to surgery, orthopedics, psychiatry, and infectious disease sent, and

(4) A complete and unswerving belief on the patient's part that his full name was Jesus Christ Crucified, Most Holy Lord, Son of God, and Savior of Righteous People; psychiatry consult initiated and labeled 'stat.'

"Listen, now, I mean it," the young cop said, stung by Cleta's failure to be impressed by him.

"You don't want to be fooling around with this joker. Don't even talk to him any more than you have to; don't be letting him run his rap on you."

Cleta hesitated in the doorway. Ordinarily she could work by the night light, a purplish fluorescent glimmer from over the room's tiny built-in sink. The stink of paraldehyde was stronger here, like glue fumes, and from the direction of the bed came a many-voiced whispering as of a churchful of people all murmuring the same prayer in not-quite unison.

Swallowing hard, she snapped on the overhead lights. The sight of the patient strapped into his bed reassured her: thick leather manacles from his wrists and ankles to the side rails, white canvas posey-vest restraining his torso to the mattress.

At least, it reassured her until the patient's lips ceased moving while the whispering went on, a good three or four seconds during which fear squeezed Cleta's throat and the sounds slowly faded. Trick, she told herself, plenty of people can talk without moving their lips. Stolidly she approached the bed.

The patient was dressed in one of Chelsea Memorial Hospital's blue-and-white cotton johnnycoats. His ropy arms stuck straight out onto the beige thermal blanket. Something was tattooed in purple on his scarred knuckles. His dark, Kwell-shampooed hair was matted damply to his head, and his eyes were closed.

"So, this bozo you're married to," he said, not opening his eyes. "Why don't you try clouting him across the chops next time he belts you one? You're big enough to do it, aren't you?"

Cleta stared. The patient had not seen her, did not know her. Certainly he had not seen the bruises. No one had—not this time, anyway.

"How . . . how did you know that?" she whispered.

The patient's eyes snapped open, pale blue rimmed with red. "I peeked," he told her. "Minor miracle. Why don't you let me out of these contraptions," he added, his fingers wriggling obscenely like nests of snakes, "and I'll tell you something more."

"Okay," the young cop stepped in, "that's enough. Just do what you're here to do and get it done with, he's not supposed to be talking to anybody."

But Cleta could only stand frozen, heart hammering in her chest, battling the insane urge to do what the patient had asked.

"Something," the patient whispered, *"better."*

"Shut up," the cop snapped. "You want to do miracles, try bringing a couple of those dead girls back."

At his words the rest of what Cleta had heard in report sprang to mind: the basement of the abandoned rowhouse tenement from which a passing AIDS outreach worker, canvassing the neighborhood with flyers and batches of clean needles for the Spanish-speaking heroin addicts, had heard screams.

The fear she had felt at her throat now pressed

stonelike on her chest. Do it, just do it and get out, Cleta told herself.

The blood pressure cuff hung loosely around the patient's biceps. With stiffened fingers she connected the cuff's rubber pressure tubing to the mercury column mounted behind the bed and began squeezing the pressure bulb, inflating the cuff.

Meanwhile, supplied with details the other nurses mercilessly had gone on telling, her mind continued offering up images of the tenement basement: Rusting chains dangling from the pipes. Emptied food cans in a moldy heap. Smoldering religious candles, and the screaming. Surgical tools had been found in that basement, and . . . other things. Cleta forced her mind's eye firmly shut.

"Not going to take my temperature?" the patient asked.

The young cop uttered a sound of disgust. Shaking herself from her unpleasant dreamlike state, she spied the thermometer on the windowsill by a pile of clean linen and some dressing kits.

Moving slowly, carefully in the cramped room, Cleta made her way to the window and paused there, gathering her wits. Directly across the street were the married medical students' quarters, a few lights still burning orangely here and there against the cheap, thin curtains. To her left stood the hospital's parking garage, a hideous sodium-lit structure hunkering over the earth as if possessing it. Seven stories down on a landscaped plot of green stood the flower vendor's stall; between this area and the hospital's main entrance curved an asphalt driveway.

"Something *good*," the patient whispered.

A dark sedan pulled up into the driveway; the car's driver got out and hurried toward the hospital entrance, vanishing under the portico and reappearing moments later with a wheelchair.

"Listen," said the young cop, "if you're not going to . . ."

The wheelchair's occupant wore a gray hat and appeared either ill or drunk, sagging sideways as he was wheeled to the car.

"Nurse," insisted the cop, his voice hardening.

"Oh, hush up," Cleta told him as the man in the raincoat let himself be hauled bonelessly from the wheelchair. "I know what I'm doing here, and I'll take whatever time I want to with it."

The cop had liked her nervousness, she realized; it made him feel important. The patient liked it, too, but his nasty tricks were no more than that. The other nurses must have been gossiping about her in front of him, that was all. To spite them both, she remained deliberately at the window.

Seven stories down, the man in the raincoat fell heavily into the car's passenger seat. As he did so, his hat tumbled from his head and rolled briskly down the circle drive. His companion seemed not to see it come to rest beneath the flower vendor's stall. After a brief, fruitless search, the wheelchair was pushed once more out of sight beneath the portico and the car driven away.

Cleta turned, brandishing the thermometer, only to find that the patient's pupils had constricted to pinpoints, his breathing grown harsh and irregular. Beads of sweat stood out on his ashen forehead, and his pulse—when she found it—was thready.

Abruptly he convulsed, straining the straps of the canvas vest. The cardiac monitor alarms flashed briefly, then stayed on.

"Get down to the nursing station right now and call a code," she told the young cop, who opened his mouth to object. "Go!"

One of the posey straps snapped as the seizures intensified. The patient's fists and heels beat a tattoo on the mattress.

Then as abruptly as they had begun the seizures stopped. The patient's head lolled sideways, his eyes rolled whitely back. Heart rate forty and dropping; respirations diminishing. Cleta heard the code cart rumbling down the hallway, the overhead page operator summoning the anesthesia resident. They would have to turn him to get the cardiac compression board under him; in preparation for this she began swiftly opening the remaining posey straps, snapping the quick releases on the leather manacles.

As she undid the last one the patient sat up smoothly, his eyes now open and alert and appearing to be—although this, of course, was not possible—entirely red. The stone of fear in her chest transformed itself to pain, clamping down with vicious suddenness. Distantly Cleta heard cardiac alarms still jangling, the code cart's rumble seeming to come from miles away.

Get out, her mind kept insisting, but the pain insisted more; she staggered and fell heavily. Heart attack, she realized with disbelief, I'm having a bad—

"Thank you *so* much," the patient said, and flew at her.

TWO

"**T**WO funerals in one day are too many funerals," said Edwina Crusoe, eyeing herself in the bedroom mirror and deciding that the black linen suit would once again have to serve. Along with a light silk blouse, the tiny square of lace in the suit's breast pocket provided enough white to keep her from being mistaken for the widow, and besides she had nothing else appropriate.

"Ouch," she said, sliding her feet into black-and-white spectator pumps. Assessing their effect, she kicked them off in favor of the patent leather. "That's another thing I hate about dressing up, it always makes my feet hurt."

"Why not wear the flat shoes?" asked Martin McIntyre, whose summer uniform of dark blue blazer, flannel slacks, white shirt, and figured tie always looked freshly tailored for him, and whose footwear never pinched that she had heard of.

"Because flats make this skirt ruck up, you see,

it's cut for—oh, never mind," she finished, abandoning the attempt to communicate such subtleties to McIntyre. He would only go on to question the wisdom of wearing the linen suit at all, whereupon she would be back to square one in the costume department. Besides, the idea that the only shoes she could walk in were the shoes that hurt was not one she wished to examine very closely, and especially not now when she was late.

Impatiently she ran a hairbrush through her short dark hair, applied lipstick to her lips, and frowned at her tan, lean-faced reflection, deciding that like the suit it would have to serve. One's own looks, after all, were rarely the important thing at a funeral unless one happened to be the main attraction, in which case one could hardly be held responsible for them.

"Let's get it over with," she said, shooing McIntyre from a chair. "You can read the sports pages later as a reward for the ordeal we're about to put ourselves through. Thank you, by the way, for coming with me to this thing."

McIntyre was tall, slim, and hawk-faced, with a dark receding hairline, thin expressive mouth, and a habitually intelligent expression that his new wife Edwina found immensely comforting.

"You're welcome," he said, "and anyway it is my husbandly duty. Sorry I couldn't make it to the morning one with you."

She put on her hat, black straw with a narrow black ribbon and a pink silk rosebud. "That's good of you, Martin, but your duties do not include being jammed into a tiny cinderblock church with no air-conditioning, no seat cushions, no elbow room, and a congregation that apparently includes the entire population of the Western world." She gave the hat a final tilt. "Whatever else Cleta Bell may or may not have had—*her* husband, by the way, was a Neanderthal—she did indeed enjoy a rich, full, and colorful religious life."

His eyebrows rose. "Lots of gospel singing and praise-the-Lords?"

Edwina's shoulders sagged at the memory. "Plus plenty of shouting, witnessing, and amening, not to mention the odd bit of speaking in tongues. I felt like the pagan at the missionaries' convention."

"Yes, well," McIntyre smiled, "that's just what you are, my dear. In fact, it's what first attracted me. Come on, Maxie."

The black cat leapt nimbly from the bed and streaked from the room, uttering hopeful syllables on the topic of a snack.

"But," McIntyre said, "this gathering we're going to . . . well. Isn't it a little early for a memorial service? As opposed to an actual funeral, I mean." Pausing in the kitchen he rummaged for the cat's sake in the refrigerator, fished around in a jar, and dropped an object to a paper plate. "There you go, boy, a nice pickled pig's foot. Yum, yum." He turned back to Edwina. "I mean, the fellow's only been dead a couple of days."

Maxie's nose wrinkled doubtfully over the thing McIntyre had dropped before him, his look conveying clearly his opinion that while marriage

13

might have improved McIntyre's diet, it most certainly had not improved his own. Male humans in the household, his frown seemed to say, ate up all the leftovers once consigned exclusively to himself, while introducing snack foods utterly foreign to his digestion. Glumly he batted at the pig's foot.

"Mmm, yes," said Edwina, plucking up the horrid relic and depositing it in the garbage bag, "it is early. But Bennett Weissman is different from Cleta Bell. First of all, he's Jewish, so they buried him before he got cold, practically. And second, all the academic medical community leaves town soon—if you want proof of that, try getting an appointment with them in August—so this is the latest that lots of people who knew him would get a chance to go." She dropped a chunk of cheddar cheese onto Maxie's plate and backed off before he could complain about it.

"How'd all these academic types get so rich they can afford to leave town in August?" McIntyre asked. "I thought only the private-practice medical people made money."

"You've got it backwards," she replied, letting him out the apartment door and producing her keys. "They were rich in the first place, and so were their fathers and grandfathers, you see. That's how they got to be academics, by being able to afford the high tuitions and ignore the measly salaries."

"Oh," he said as they waited in the outer foyer for the elevator to arrive, "so this is some snooty kind of shindig we're going to?" He glanced unhappily down at his blazer and slacks, which were as usual immaculate. Then the elevator doors slid open and he allowed her to precede him into the car.

As he did so, Edwina regarded her husband with affectionate amusement, unable to think of a person better able or less eager to subject himself to shindigs of any sort, for—like his brains and his looks—Martin McIntyre's manners and common sense had apparently been hard-wired into him at birth and had never been known to fail. "Exceedingly snooty," she assured him.

That Bennett Weissman had ended his own life did not squelch the pleasure his friends took in the brilliant day. That he had done it by blowing his brains out while sitting in the front seat of his exhaust-filled automobile seemed to them inexplicable, but even so not particularly deserving of criticism. Bennett, most of them felt, was a sensible man and so must have had his reasons; it was not for them to judge, and in any case he had at least been thorough about the thing.

Thus the mood at the reception following Weissman's memorial service was subdued but not gloomy, as people stood about eating tiny sandwiches, sipping drinks, and enjoying the long, green lawn that sloped down to the sparkling expanse of salt water behind Weissman's huge house.

"Terrible thing about the nurse," said Harry Lemon, munching reflectively on a petit four as he gazed out over the waves of Long Island

Sound. "You could see it coming, of course, she must have weighed a good three hundred pounds."

Harry himself was plump and purse-lipped, his bald head gleaming pinkly from beneath a few remaining wisps of blond hair. It was Harry who, as chief medical officer on the ward at Chelsea Memorial Hospital just four nights ago, had directed the luckless attempts at resuscitating Cleta Bell.

"Just getting her out into the hall where we could work on her was a horror show," he said. Reaching for another dainty item from the silver tray being circulated by a waiter, he caught himself at it and picked up his glass of seltzer water instead.

"I heard she was frightened to death," said Edwina, sipping from her own glass of lemonade. She had known and liked Bennett Weissman well enough in a casual way, but not well enough to get tipsy over him in the middle of the afternoon. Glancing about at the crowd of mourners milling on the lawn and gathering by the drinks table, however, she noted that in other quarters sorrows were already being rather heavily drowned.

"That's the gossip among the nurses who were there, you know, that the patient somehow . . ." she paused, catching sight of McIntyre, who was nodding gravely at something a very old lady in a gray silk dress was telling him. Let's wind it down and get out of here, she thought at him, and he tipped his head minutely at her in reply.

"Scared the life out of her," Harry agreed, "and

he came near to scaring the life out of me, too, I'll tell you. Perched on the foot of the bed like some enormous vampire bat, full-bore psychotic and screaming his bloody head off—in Latin, no less. It took six people to wrestle him down and get him sedated."

A few feet away by the garden wall a pale young woman stood alone, wearing a plain white blouse, navy skirt, and saddle shoes, and looking as if she would rather be anywhere else. A breeze off the water ruffled her short mousy hair; she brushed it from her face irritably.

"At any rate I must get back to the hospital," said Harry. "Poor old Bennett, he was an awfully decent fellow. Good doctor, too, back when he was still in practice. I'll never understand why he decided to take on that magazine. I suppose it put a lot of pressure on him."

"I suppose," murmured Edwina, thinking that editing a small medical journal, however well regarded, was hardly the sort of job to inspire one to put a bullet through one's head; one could, after all, always quit.

Then a thought struck her. "Harry, what was he saying in Latin?"

But Harry was already toddling rotundly away, returning to his rounds and his patients and the squads of residents, interns, and medical students whom he supervised long-sufferingly but with immense devotion and expertise. Turning, she found that the unhappy girl had vanished— belatedly, Edwina recognized her as Bennett Weissman's daughter Mona—although the opportunity to do a good deed had not, she realized, as with sinking heart she watched a tall, cadaverous fellow striding determinedly across the lawn at her, carrying two glasses of what looked like champagne.

"Hello, Carlton," she greeted him warmly as he loomed over her, proffering a glass which she refused.

"Always a pleasure, Edwina, even in sad times," Carlton Keene intoned, his hunched posture and brooding expression making him resemble, as usual, some large dark bird of prey. He was sweet on her, she knew, and for years had been admiring her from afar. Fortunately, however, he was also brilliant, busy, and possessed of a large and successful dermatology practice, as well as of a wife whose faithfulness to him was legend and of more children than even he could really afford, all of whom adored him extravagantly.

If not for these things, Carlton had assured her more than once, he would swoop down and spirit Edwina away with him—both of them of course knowing full well that he would not do any such thing, and that he was in truth relieved not to have to do so.

"Marriage," he intoned, "has only made you more beautiful. I do wish you every possible happiness, my dear."

"Thank you, Carlton," she replied, feeling the intensity of his regard like an unwanted spotlight. But she did not wish to offend him; his warmth, while embarrassing, was sincere and his feelings were sensitive. "It's kind of you to say so. But what will happen to the journal, now that Bennett's gone? Will you be editing in the interim? Or permanently?"

"Good god, no." Carlton swallowed some champagne. "There's a committee set up to find a new editor. New issue's shipped and the next's already in galleys. Have to hand it to old Bennett, he left things well fixed. And it's never been a problem finding contributors. People are dying to get in."

He frowned as his own words struck him. "Anxious to get in, I mean," he amended. "Anyway, I was never involved in the hands-on editing, just in recruiting reviewers. Experts, you know, who say whether or not a proposed article is any good, comment on the science, the logic, the writing, and so on. Only Bennett knew the nuts and bolts of putting the magazine together. We'll be in a bind there, if the committee doesn't come up with someone soon."

"Really." Edwina sipped lemonade. Across the lawn she saw McIntyre pause by Mona Weissman, alone and still languishing as if invisible amid the crowd of her late father's friends and associates. With the swiftness of long experience, McIntyre summed her up at a glance and engaged her in conversation.

Good old Martin, she thought, then saw the girl seem to turn if possible even paler than before at something McIntyre said.

"Bullet through his head," said Carlton Keene morosely, his gaze lingering now on the sparkling blue horizon beyond Bennett Weissman's garden wall. "Who would have thought it of him? The most unlikely suicide, I'd have believed. How little we know our friends." He sighed. "I'll miss the old gadfly."

"Yes, I suppose," Edwina replied distractedly, realizing what McIntyre must have said, and then what she had just said. "Oh, Carlton, I'm sorry, of course you'll miss him. I meant I suppose we don't know our friends the way we think. My sympathies, Carlton, really, but now I see my husband is beckoning me. I must leave soon, and I haven't even spoken to Mrs. Weissman yet."

Carlton Keene took her hand in his pale, chilly one. "Edwina, I hope that fellow knows what a lucky man he is."

"Thank you," she said, managing a smile, "I'll be sure to let him know you said so."

But as she drew back her hand she could not help wondering whether, in addition to being a lucky man, McIntyre had not just now also been an indiscreet one. Mona Weissman was drawing him urgently toward the house, an enormous fieldstone structure with green-painted shutters and geranium-filled windowboxes freshly gleaming in the afternoon sun.

Edwina's progress across the lawn was impeded by the number of persons who stopped her to say hello—fifteen years of nursing followed by the establishment of her own consulting agency had made her name and face well known in clinical and academic medical circles—and by the heels of the impractical patent leather shoes, which punctured the turf at every step.

At last she managed to extricate herself from yet another pressing invitation; most of the people here, it seemed, planned on going to dinner somewhere pleasant and would like nothing better than to have Edwina join them—mostly, she suspected, in order to meet McIntyre, about whose person and profession there existed great curiosity. That she had married at all they found surprising, for Edwina's resistance to romantic blandishments had been legend, but that she had married a homicide detective was in the way of being a sensation.

Her own curiosity, however, had principally to do with her husband's location right this minute, since at last glimpse he had been entering the house with a weeping Mona Weissman clinging helplessly to his arm.

"His *hat*," Mona Weissman sobbed, "my father didn't have on his *hat* and he *wouldn't* have . . ."

The room was a study in polished hardwood and burnished brass, tall casement windows overlooking professional plantings of laurel, azalea, and rhododendron. The curtains were sea green, the carpets gold wool, the chairs upholstered in beige, nubbly fabric straight out of a decorator's swatch book. It all looked just about as lived-in as a department store window and nowhere near as comfortable.

"Now, now," said McIntyre, offering his handkerchief. But like others of his gender he privately regarded all weeping women as anathema; spying Edwina he stepped back quickly and gratefully.

Meanwhile since Mona's argument seemed to be that hatlessness deterred suicide, Edwina was inclined at once to discount it. She, after all, was wearing a hat this very moment, but removing it would not prevent her thinking wistfully of gas, a fatal dose of which she would rather inhale than listen to what she was listening to.

It was not that she lacked sympathy for poor Mona. But the young woman was the second person in just half an hour to suggest that Bennett Weissman had not committed suicide, or at least that if he had, the act had been entirely unexpected. And not one of those to whom she had spoken outside, Edwina now realized, had said or even hinted that they had seen it coming.

All of which she regarded as an ominous sign. Persons planning to end their own existences, in Edwina's professional experience, rarely failed to warn their nearest and dearest; not all of them, perhaps, and perhaps not always very intelligibly, but in retrospect, at least, almost always purposefully. They gave away possessions, made dark remarks, put business or financial affairs in order, and in general prepared the rest of the world for their imminent demise. Sometimes they even wrote suicide notes.

Bennett Weissman had left no note, dropped no hints, and disposed of no possessions. His money and professional affairs were in good order, as was his personal life as far as anyone knew; there had been, at least, no whispers among the survivors on the lawn. Bennett had simply driven home late a few nights ago from his office at Chelsea Memorial Hospital—as physician-in-chief emeritus he retained a space in the old clinic wing there, along with funding for a secretary—drunk most of a bottle of twelve-year-old bourbon, run a length of washing-machine hose from the exhaust pipe of his car to the nearly closed vent window, and shut the garage door.

In the car he had settled back into the driver's seat before starting the engine, activating the automatic door locks, turning the radio to a classical music station, and firing a .22-caliber bullet from a handgun he kept in a desk drawer against prowlers into his own erudite and amusing brain, a feat requiring that the weapon be held—for a moment, anyway—at quite a steep and awkward angle.

A .22 was hardly the instrument of choice for such a task in any case; too easy, with it, to abolish the brain's higher functions while sparing the vegetative ones, thus providing oneself with an extremely good motive for suicide while removing, permanently and completely, all possibility of another try at it.

Still, a .22 was what Weissman had owned and he had not, apparently, forgotten his cranial anatomy, nor had his aim been shaky in the final moment. The exhaust pipe was obviously for insurance, in case he missed, but he hadn't missed.

All these facts clicked rapidly through Edwina's mind as she watched poor mousy little Mona Weissman weeping and heard the girl's disjointed but oddly convincing litany of complaints.

". . . didn't *drink*," she sobbed, "not in trouble or sad or rejected or even running out of money. The family was fine, his friends adored him, and if he had enemies they were too embarrassed to say so, they knew no one would believe anything bad about—"

"Enemies?" Edwina cut in. "*Did* your father have enemies?" From the casement window where he had seemed to be ignoring the whole conversation, McIntyre turned casually but with interest, too.

Mona's sobs shut off like a sharply twisted faucet. Seeing the handkerchief in her hand she dabbed her eyes with it, thought another moment, and gave it a brisk, efficient blow.

"Oh, thank you," she said with a face like sunshine breaking through rain. "I was sure if you would only *listen* to me—"

"Mona," cut in an angry voice from the doorway. "Mona, you foolish girl. I knew it was wrong to let you be here talking to people. What in the world have you been saying to them?"

The woman in the doorway was tall, flaxen haired, and highly polished, dressed in a flowing silk caftan of deepest navy blue. The ruin of her face was not so much from age; rather, botched plastic surgery and widespread collagen collapse had transformed what might otherwise have been venerable into something like an abandoned construction site. Aristocratic in manner and posture, Serina Weissman conveyed no very crushing grief in her dark-eyed gaze, or in fact in any other way.

"Do please accept my sympathies," Edwina ventured. "We all will miss Dr. Weissman very much."

"Indeed," Mrs. Weissman snapped unpleasantly, "how touching. I'm sure it will comfort me hugely in the nights ahead. Nights," she added, "which dear Bennett has so carefully arranged for me."

At her angry gesture Mona jumped as if jerked by a string. "Come along," Mrs. Weissman said scathingly, "you've bothered our guests quite enough with your weeping and your silliness. Why can't I trust you to do one single thing correctly, and on this of all days? Sometimes I think the doctors were right and there is something wrong with you. Your father would never believe that, of course, but your father is dead, now. You would do well," she finished in tones of vague threat, "to keep that fact in mind."

At her words the inward collapse of Mona Weissman was one of the wretchedest things Edwina had ever seen; it was then she came to her decision.

Mrs. Weissman tapped her foot. "Well?" she demanded. "Are you coming? Please don't force me to lose my temper with you."

"I'm very sorry," Mona whispered, getting to her feet.

"Good." Serina Weissman's face showed satisfaction. "I'm glad you can display some shred of sense. You might as well go out to the kitchen and help the caterers put away the—"

"Mona," Edwina cut in, "I gather my husband has mentioned to you who I am?" McIntyre's glance confirmed this. "And that, I suppose, is why you began relating your suspicions to him?"

"Yes," she admitted with a fearful glance at her mother, "but I'm awfully sorry, I didn't mean to . . ."

"Very well." Edwina drew a card from her handbag. "I'll see you tomorrow morning in my office. To explain to me further," she finished, uncharitably enjoying Mrs. Weissman's look of outrage, "how I ought to begin investigating your father's death, which I shall of course take on as a case of murder."

THREE

AT seven o'clock on an August morning, New Haven was not yet the stinking steambath of heat, humidity, and sun-drenched hydrocarbons it would later become. The breeze off the harbor was cool and sweet, the sunshine pale yellow and gently promising, and nothing had yet had time to go very wrong.

Seated with McIntyre on the screened, shaded balcony of their apartment, gazing out over the city and the water beyond, Edwina sipped coffee and hoped Bennett Weissman had killed himself, and that she would find this out for sure within a few hours or days.

McIntyre at least was convinced that she would. Yet she continued to feel an obscure, pre-monitory tingle, like the first faint itch of some virulent, soon-to-be-developed rash.

"Just because you are a homicide detective," she told her husband as he swallowed his orange juice, "doesn't mean you're infallible on the sub-ject of murder."

He looked up in mild agreement. "If it did, I would know what to do about Craig Fellowes, wouldn't I? The one who killed all those women on Beers Street, apparently," he explained.

She put down her coffee cup. "Good heavens, he's yours? Can't you get rid of him?"

But of course he couldn't; the nastiest cases always seemed to go to McIntyre, whose habit of clearing them with a minimum of further nastiness was well known. "And what do you mean, 'apparently'? The newspapers at least seem to think it's obvious he did it."

McIntyre chewed the last bite of his raisin toast, washed it down with the last of his glass of milk. His routine of eating a meal first thing in the morning was just one of the husbandly quirks she was having to get used to; averting her eye she poured herself another cup of coffee and took a reluctant nibble of the croissant he had urged upon her.

"Mere obviousness is not accepted in the courtroom," he noted. "What I need is evidence. Specifically, at the moment, evidence that shows he isn't sick—physically, mentally, or in any other way that would keep him from participating effectively in his own defense. Evidence the DA can present to the judge."

"Oh, of course, I see. And then what happens?" The morning air began thickening with heat and haze; distant sirens began screaming somewhere in the city.

"If I win we go to trial and Fellowes gets convicted, I hope and pray, on fourteen—so far—

counts of murder with depraved, and never sees the light of day again except through a pattern of iron bars."

McIntyre touched a napkin to his lips and got up. "But if the defense wins," he went on, "Craig Fellowes gets committed to Whiting Forensics Institute, where they drug him into a shambling stupor and train him to give the right answers to the questions they're going to keep asking him. Questions like what day is it, where are you, what's your name, and who's the president."

"And when he does answer them correctly?"

McIntyre shrugged. "Then he comes back and gets tried for the murders. But by that time, you see, he'll probably have been a maximum-security mental patient for twelve to sixteen months, and a jury will figure if he was that sick after the events, then he was probably sick during them, too. Not guilty by reason of."

"So he'll get sent back to the hospital."

"Precisely. From which, due to the miracles of psychiatry, even he will eventually be released on medication, which he will of course stop taking—these bozos always stop taking, a voice from God or a band of angels or something will come and *order* him to stop taking—and then he'll vanish. And no one will ever hear of him again until another bunch of bodies shows up in another tenement basement in, I hope, some other city somewhere."

"Oh," said Edwina. "But, Martin, if he thinks he's Jesus Christ," this also having been in the newspapers, "how can you . . . ?"

McIntyre smiled grimly. "I don't care if he thinks he's the rotor on a cartoon beanie, he chopped those girls up and then he hid their body parts, which means he knew it was wrong. And once I interrupt his program with that little message, I'll bet old Craig stops flapping his wings and starts talking sensibly, or at least sensibly compared to what he was spouting off last night."

"Which was?" Edwina gave up and ate the remainder of the croissant rather than hear again about how breakfast was the most important meal of the day. Surprisingly, it tasted good.

"That his fiery wrath," McIntyre replied, "would burn the Whalley Avenue jail right down to its foundations—that, not by coincidence, is where he is now being confined—unless we gave him a thousand dollars and set him free by midnight last night."

As he spoke, the telephone in the dining room began ringing. While he went to answer it she regarded another croissant, broke it experimentally into two pieces, and began buttering one of them. She had eaten the first and was starting in on the second—daringly this time, with a dab of marmalade—when he returned to the balcony, his expression stunned and disbelieving.

"That was the office," he said slowly. "There's a four-alarm fire burning out of control, down at the Whalley jail."

Half an hour later at the nursing station on the seventh floor of Chelsea Memorial Hospital, Harry Lemon lowered his face into his hands.

Before him on the nursing desk lay an open chart, its pages scribbled thickly with consult notes. Edwina did not know the patient whose ailments this chart concerned, but Harry did—to Harry's sorrow, judging by his expression.

Beside the chart lay a fat, legal-looking envelope. Edwina had been about to tell Harry about the fire and Craig Fellowes' prediction of it, but after a look at Harry she decided not to.

"Bleach," he said tonelessly while Edwina ran her eye over the chart. There were comments from the departments of peripheral vascular surgery, infectious disease, general surgery, radiology . . .

"Harry, it looks as if the whole hospital's worked on this patient already. What are you, the court of last resort?"

"He was my patient in the first place," Harry replied in tones of glum resignation, "and now he is again. Rather, he's a patient on my service. I won't be caring for him directly, I have just been informed. Whoopee," he twirled his finger in the air, "and to think I gave up a promising veterinary career."

For Harry such downheartedness was unusual indeed. He dealt regularly with diseases ranging from the malignant to the obscene, beating them back with a potent combination of medical artillery and sheer personal outrage. Edwina remembered him once crouched by a dying patient's bedside while the final infusion of chemotherapy ran in, shouting insults at the patient on the theory that anger-triggered hormones might somehow boost the chemo's effectiveness. For this Harry had endured the intense and dripping scorn of the patient's nurses, all of whom were forced to apologize to Harry on the day two weeks later when the patient walked out of the hospital.

"Bleach," he said again, "is virucidal. It kills, as we all know, the AIDS virus. And my patient here, who is perhaps the most ignorant and degenerate bit of allegedly human protoplasm it has ever been my misfortune to encounter—I'm sorry, Edwina, but my patients aren't all saints, you know, and this fellow is the moral equivalent of a tapeworm—well, at any rate this patient knows it, too."

"He knows bleach kills the AIDS virus," Edwina said, beginning unhappily to suspect what might be coming.

Harry nodded. "We instructed him carefully, last time we discharged him. At which time, after six whole weeks of intense work on him, he was in good shape. Eating, getting around, and feeling good. So, we told him, clean your needles—it was too much to hope for that he might not go back to shooting up, but at least we could keep him from infecting other people—"

"Clean them," said Edwina, "with bleach." All around her the controlled chaos of the medical ward continued: blinking call lights, scurrying technicians, ringing phones, and the rumble of the portable X-ray machine. A nurse plucked a chart from the chart rack, scanned it, and slapped it back, muttering something about people who couldn't be bothered renewing medication orders.

Harry sighed, reaching for the offending chart. "Right," he said, scribbling in the front section of the plastic folder. Reading what he had written, he frowned and scribbled a bit more.

"So," he went on, signing his name in a lavish scrawl, "he got some bleach and cleaned up all his needles, and then he got the bright idea to shoot him*self* up with this miracle cleansing fluid. After all, if it works for needles, why not on his body? And for good measure he swallowed a pint of it, too."

"Oh, my god," Edwina said. "What happened to him?"

"Sloughed the muscle mass off his arms, killed his kidneys, and vulcanized his lung tissues. The only thing he didn't manage to kill was his bad attitude, which at this point is what's keeping him alive."

Harry slid the chart back into the rack. "Now most of his large, vocal family are furious with me because I didn't warn him that shooting up with bleach might be dangerous to his health."

He made a sound of disgust. "Of course, I didn't tell him not to stick beans up his nose, either, for which I suppose I am also going to be sued." He waved at the legal envelope.

"Oh, Harry." She sat down beside him. "That's not fair. Who would ever even have the gall to try such a—"

"Paul Driefield would, and I'm not being sued

for fairness. I'm being sued for money. Huge sums," he emphasized, "of money."

"Oh, dear. Isn't Driefield the one with all the—"

"Absolutely." Harry's nod was hopeless. "Defender of the downtrodden. Sticker-upper for the socially disenfranchised. Driefield's whole law firm's nothing but an ongoing pep rally for the fashionably persecuted, and he knows how to massage the press. He'll be on the front page for days with this, and I'll end up looking like Dr. Mengele."

Edwina stood up. "No, you won't, Harry," she told him.

"Sometimes," he went on miserably, "I wonder why we doctors don't just pay our malpractice premiums to the lawyers. Cheaper that way, you know, we could cut out the middleman and forget the patients entirely."

"Harry," she repeated, "no, you won't." Tearing a history-and-progress sheet from a pad, she wrote down a telephone number.

"Call this fellow—Hansford Meredith. Tell him I sent you. He'll help you."

Harry regarded the number doubtfully. "Thank you, Edwina. I appreciate it. But the medical association's given me a local fellow to call, someone who knows the—"

"Harry," she interrupted him briskly, because what Harry needed now was not the medical association's pet lawyer, however well meaning or experienced. What Harry needed was a shark, someone with big sharp teeth and no qualms about biting with them.

"Harry, remember a couple of years ago there was a woman doctor up at Wellington Hospital who got sued? One of her patients said she hadn't instructed him properly, said he lost the use of his legs because of this woman's negligence?"

"Indeed," Harry frowned, "and she had quite an unorthodox life-style. Ran some sort of commune and owned a hundred or so dogs and cats on a lot of acreage way up in the Litchfield hills somewhere. Funny, though, I don't remember much more of it."

"Precisely," she replied. "That's my point. The specific thing for which she neglected to give instructions was a private habit the patient had. One she never knew of, but Driefield argued that she ought to have. It involved, as I recall, lengths of clothesline and a leather outfit." She paused delicately.

"Ah, yes." Harry remembered now. "Once the details of the story came out, the claimant turned out to be quite an unsavory fellow, and his family was no great shakes either. Their names and faces turned up in all the tabloids, and after that . . ."

A look of enlightenment spread on Harry's face. "Oh. Yes, of course I do see. Driefield represented the plaintiff, and Meredith the defendant."

He frowned down at the number again. "I recall thinking," he went on, "that perhaps the physician was to blame, at least in part. It was, after all, a narcotic drug she prescribed. She might have suspected he would be tempted to abuse it, even without knowing all his pathological details. He was her long-time patient, she must have had some idea about him."

Edwina sighed inwardly. What Harry said was true, but it was beside the point. "I know, you're supposed to use good judgment when you take care of sick people. But now what are you supposed to do, tie yourself to the railroad tracks because you didn't happen to be clairvoyant enough that day?"

Harry looked up, his face elementally troubled. "I don't know," he said. "Maybe I should have realized what he would think about that bleach, maybe I ought to have warned him. I did tell him to rinse the needles. But maybe his complete stupidity is part of his pathology and I ought to have known that, and done something about treating it."

And that in a nutshell was the thing about taking care of people: what you did made a real and physical difference to a real, physical person, and sometimes despite your best efforts the difference turned out badly. It was the price, Edwina thought, of doing anything.

"Harry," she said, "it's not about you and the patient anymore. It's about you and Paul Driefield. Just keep that in mind, and call the number."

She turned to go, then remembered what she had come for. "Oh, and I had a question to ask you."

Looking battered but unbowed, Harry Lemon nodded, supplying her at once with directions through the medical center to Bennett Weissman's office.

"He often worked late," said Marcia Larsen, looking up from her desk in the smaller of the office suite's two rooms. Beyond the secretary's chamber was what looked like the consulting room of an old-fashioned general practitioner, its oaken desk and worn leather armchair centered on a threadbare Persian carpet. On the walls hung diplomas, certificates, photographs, and a matted, framed cover of *Clinical Communications*, the medical journal Bennett Weissman had founded and edited.

"I think he probably didn't want to go home," Marcia Larsen said, her fingers moving practicedly on the keys of her typewriter. Arrayed on the desk before her were the tools of her trade: paper clips, White-Out, pens, pencils and erasers, a pink pad of While You Were Out slips, a Rolodex, and an open appointment calendar.

The air in the old clinic building, which now housed more secretaries' desks than patient care areas, was rich with the smells of floor polish, wet paint, and ozone from the overworked copying machines. On Weissman's door was mounted a brass nameplate engraved in flowing script; in his mullioned window overlooking a small green courtyard an old GE fan whirred its rotating wire head, its breeze lightly riffling the papers on his desk. As Edwina watched, a few of the papers flew up, scattering themselves across the carpet.

"I think," said Marcia Larsen, "his wife drove him to it." She rapped out a final few words and snapped the sheet of paper from her typewriter. "To overwork, I mean."

"Really," said Edwina. Marcia Larsen was perhaps forty-five years old, with iron-gray hair wrapped into a chignon and black horn-rimmed glasses through which she peered intently. She wore a white eyelet blouse and gathered denim skirt, sensible canvas shoes, and a wedding ring with diamond chips set into it.

"Someone," said Marcia Larsen, "should have told her so."

Propped up beside the typewriter was a manuscript heavily marked in blue pencil. Mrs. Larsen was typing a clean copy of it, frowning as she deciphered the marks and interpolated them.

"But no one had the nerve," she went on as the typewriter clattered on a new sheet. "Sit down, I can talk and type at the same time." She jerked her head at a straight chair across from her desk. "What did you say your name was?"

Repeating it, Edwina seated herself. "His daughter," she lied smoothly, "asked me to gather some information. For the insurance investigators, you know, so that Dr. Weissman's affairs can be concluded smoothly."

Mrs. Larsen shot a glance of undeceived acuity at Edwina. "Mona? I'm surprised she could string enough words together to ask anything. What few brains she has don't work very well most of the time. I met her once, and I assure you once was enough."

It occurred to Edwina that Bennett Weissman hadn't hired a fool to run his office or help put out his medical journal. And Marcia Larsen had worked for Weissman for twenty years—Edwina had glimpsed her the day before at the memorial gathering but had not chanced to speak with her—which meant, very likely, that she no more believed the story of the insurance investigators than she thought she could jump out the mullioned window and fly.

"Mrs. Larsen," said Edwina, "Mona told me she didn't think her father had killed himself. She's asked me to investigate the idea. I'm not sure yet why I believe she might be right, but I'll be seeing her at ten this morning. The truth is, I wondered if before I do see her you might tell me something to help put Bennett Weissman in perspective for me."

Mrs. Larsen turned off the typewriter and stared down at her hands. They were tan and capable looking, with scrubbed, square-clipped nails and the slightly ragged cuticles of the weekend gardener. When she looked up her eyes were full of tears.

"When my husband died, Dr. Weissman paid off the mortgage on my house. He never said he was doing it, and he never took any payment from me. He just went down to the bank and talked to the bank manager. A few days later I got the mortgage stamped 'Paid.' "

She wiped her eyes with a tissue. "That was the

way he did things, you see. When he started up the journal, neither of us knew a thing about running one. But he said, 'Marcia, we'll just learn as we go on.' And we did.''

She smiled wanly, remembering. "We used to have, oh, such a wonderful time. Funny little things would happen. Once we ran a limerick contest, and of course a medical journal is supposed to be much too serious for that. Do you know, we got limericks from some of the most eminent doctors in the world, wanting to win the prize? After that we had to do it every year, the demand was so great for it.''

She paused. "They're really all poets at heart, you know, or painters or musicians. I sometimes see them in their white coats hurrying by, or I have to speak with them. Arrogant, you know, or impatient. But it's all right. I understand.''

Edwina tipped her head. "I'm afraid I don't quite follow.''

Marcia Larsen shrugged. "Well, what they've all given up, you see. Everyone thinks of doctors as having lots of money and being so powerful and important. But almost every one of them wanted to be something else. And instead they went to medical school and the responsibility got them, and here they are.''

She sighed, aimlessly arranging small items on her desk. "It always does get them, if they're any good. And of course the fascination. Once you've learned a little bit about it, medicine is rather like a mystery story, with clues and villains and red herrings. You keep wanting to follow it, even I do.

If you're a person with any natural curiosity, I mean."

Edwina, whose view of the medical profession was a good deal less romantic than Marcia Larsen's, thought unfulfilled career ambitions hardly excused the sort of rudeness the secretary must meet with regularly. She was not quite the passive kick-me sort who invited true abuse, but it was easy to imagine her backing off when she ought to have been delivering a blistering reply.

With a final sniff Mrs. Larsen shut the tissue box back into the desk drawer. "And that is one reason why I'm rather glad you stopped by, Miss Crusoe."

She locked the drawer and got up from behind her desk. "You see, for all I think Mona Weissman is a silly little twit, as bad as her mother in her way, I must say I also think that for once she seems to have come up with a reasonable idea."

Edwina blinked. Marcia Larsen picked up her purse and glanced about the little office.

"You mean," Edwina said, "you don't think he shot himself?"

"Murder is not an idea that springs readily to mind." Marcia Larsen shut off the fan in Weissman's window. "Not in connection with Dr. Weissman."

Closing the door between the inner and outer offices, she produced a ring of keys and applied one to the brass Schlage lock with which the oaken door had been fitted—and fitted recently, too, Edwina thought. Above the untarnished hardware, Weissman's nameplate glimmered venerably in contrast.

"At least," Mrs. Larsen amended with a penetrating glance at Edwina, "it was not an idea that sprang readily to my mind. But now that it's in someone else's . . ."

She looked unhappily about the room as if memorizing it, as if when she came back she wanted to know at once whether anybody else had been there.

Or perhaps still was there, waiting for her. The idea felt right the instant it occurred to Edwina, for Marcia Larsen's air of quiet competence was marred by just one thing: the look in her eyes, showing clearly that the idea of murder had not only sprung to her mind, but was in fact still actively preying upon it.

"Would you like to come with me for a cup of coffee, Miss Crusoe?" the secretary invited. "If you're going to become involved in Dr. Weissman's death, there are a few things about his life that you might want to know."

The cafeteria nearest the clinic building was in the medical school; to reach it they followed a tangled route of corridors, stairways, and propped-open fire doors bearing signs that warned KEEP CLOSED, until at last they reached the street.

Here the morning sun glared down mercilessly, whitening the sidewalks and dazzling Edwina's eyes. Graduate students in shorts and tank tops lugged backpacks up the broad marble steps of the library, hurrying toward the air-conditioned comfort of the stacks. Vendors under blue-striped umbrellas sold the first cold sodas of the day, plunging their hands into vats of melting ice to fish out the dripping bottles.

"I wait so eagerly for summer," Marcia Larsen remarked as they passed into the shade of the medical school building, "but once it arrives I know again it's really spring I cared for."

Inside, the first chill blast of the air-conditioning made them sigh in relief. "Now I suppose I'll be wishing I'd brought a sweater," the secretary laughed, but her face was worried again by the time they had carried their coffees to a table.

"I'm really quite glad to see you," she began when they were seated, "because, you see, I've been thinking it, too. That he wouldn't—didn't—shoot himself. Only I'm afraid I was too cowardly to say it, especially when no one else was saying it. Being only the secretary, you know, and then . . . well. In many ways I do fear I'm not as forceful a person as I ought to be."

"Why wouldn't he shoot himself?" Edwina asked. "And have you any idea, if he didn't, who might have?"

Marcia Larsen looked miserable. "Miss Crusoe, what I'm about to tell you . . . well. I've read about you in the newspapers, that kidnapped little girl and those deaths on the medical wards."

Edwina nodded. In her bag was a packet of business cards, one of which she had given to Mona Weissman: Edwina Crusoe, R.N., Confidential Consulting, and in smaller type below;

Medical/Health Matters Only. After retiring while still in her early thirties from nursing at Chelsea Memorial Hospital, she had specialized at first in tripping up the quacks, fakes, hucksters, snake-oil salesmen, and shameless shenanigans promoters who infested the medical profession just as frequently as they did any other.

Lately, though, she had unmasked several murderers, and of course this had been in the newspapers—to Edwina's continuing annoyance, anonymity being much handier for snooping purposes.

"So," Marcia Larsen continued, "you may learn this on your own. Although I don't know how. We were very careful."

"I see," said Edwina as enlightenment dawned.

Mrs. Larsen glanced around anxiously, to see that no tables within hearing distance were occupied.

"We were . . . involved," she finished in a near whisper. "For more than ten years, after my husband died." She took a nervous gulp of her coffee. "I hope you don't think I'm terrible."

Edwina considered briefly. "No, I don't," she said. "And in any case it's not my business to judge you."

"It started out so innocently," Marcia went on. "He liked dahlias, I have lots of them in my garden, and one day he stopped by to see some new ones I'd just gotten from Rhode Island."

She smiled, remembering. "After a while I had

to set aside a special plot for him. He loved digging around in the dirt and at home they had a gardener. He said he didn't dare touch things in the yard there for fear of spoiling something expensive. But he didn't want a divorce and I had no desire to be married again. So we just went on that way, quite happily. Until . . ."

Her face pinched. "Until he found out he was ill. A rare form of bone cancer."

Edwina blinked inwardly. No one had mentioned this.

"And of course I was horrified, but he said I mustn't worry," Marcia Larsen went on. "He'd be needing treatments but they would be no worse than a bad case of flu. I'd have to run the magazine during those times, but in between, he said, he would be perfectly all right. The five-year survival rate for what he had, he told me, was better than seventy percent."

"How comforting," said Edwina without trying to disguise her tone.

"Yes," said Marcia with a quick little glance of gratitude. "It meant a three-in-ten chance of being dead. I'd read medical manuscripts enough to know it was going to be a fight. But he insisted on seeing it simply as a project. Only, he said it made him realize that some things about his life needed changing."

Edwina sipped her cooling coffee, glanced about the room. It was past nine and the cafeteria was getting busier: white-coated lab techs, clerks in their summer dresses, haggard-eyed interns, and surgical residents in scrub suits milled about.

The medical cafeterias always reminded her of mealtimes at her old boarding school: the jostling of chairs and babbling of many voices, the steam-table smells, molded plastic trays, and the all-in-it-together sense of camaraderie that she had longed, so stubbornly and desperately, to escape.

And here I am again, she thought with a small inward laugh. Still, being able to leave when one wished made all the difference. "So he was going to do it," she said. "After all this time he was going to divorce Serina Weissman and make an honest woman out of you." She put a tinge of irony in the phrase, hoping somehow to express the sympathy she felt.

Marcia Larsen smiled, relaxing slightly, glad for a chance to talk about it with someone. "So he said, but I said since we'd never had to endure one another for more than twenty-four hours at a time, we ought to take a short trip together and see if we could tolerate each other for that long before he made any big decisions. And if that worked out, I told him, I'd think about the rest of it."

"And he agreed? When was that, exactly?"

"The day he died. I'd brought brochures for him to look at, folders and so on about places I thought we might like to visit. But the galleys for the issue were due to go back to the printer that day, and he was on the telephone all afternoon. When I left he hadn't even opened the brochures yet."

Her look softened. "That was just like Bennett, of course."

Edwina got up. "You left at your usual time that day? When is that, five o'clock or so?" They deposited their Styrofoam cups in the trash bins by the cafeteria's exit and went out.

"No," Marcia Larsen said, "nearer seven. There were quite a few letters I had to type, and I wanted to finish with them. And there's no one waiting for me to fix supper, so I've become accustomed to getting home anytime I please. On quieter days, I leave off early."

They stepped back into the steamy street. "But the thing is," she went on, blinking in the sun's glare, "Bennett didn't simply wish to marry me, he intended to marry me. He'd made that very plain, despite my doubts, and he wasn't about to change his mind. And while illness might be a suicide motive for some, it was not one for Bennett Weissman. On the contrary, do you see?"

"Yes. Of course I understand." The day was brutal; Edwina felt perspiration forming at her hairline and brushed it away. "You mentioned some problem with the issue, something Dr. Weissman was on the phone about. Was that anything serious?"

The secretary shook her head impatiently. "Oh, heavens, no, it was one of the reviewers, he'd criticized one of the journal articles severely and now he'd got his back up because the piece was running at all. He called several times, each time getting more upset because his orders weren't being followed. Bennett kept trying to smooth his feathers; he didn't want to lose him."

They paused at the entrance to the clinic building. "Is that usual?" Edwina asked. "I thought reviewers for medical journals gave criticism, not orders."

Marcia Larsen laughed ruefully. "Yes, well, try telling some of them that. And this one's the worst: he doesn't think he's a painter or musician. He thinks he's an editor."

Her face grew serious once more. "At any rate let me know if I can help, but I'd appreciate my name being left out of it, if possible. It could only cause pain to his family, you see."

"Of course," Edwina told her, beginning to feel a little stunned by the heat as she bid the secretary good-bye.

Marcia Larsen, she thought as she walked the few blocks back to her apartment, was a lucky find: pleasant, well informed, and apparently honest. Something more than she'd mentioned did seem to be worrying her, to be sure; her troubled behavior in the office still struck Edwina as odd. But she did not seem to have spared herself in her account of her affair with a married man— an affair she seemed prepared to expose, if need be, to help answer questions about that man's death.

But thirty minutes later Edwina was forced, unhappily, to revise her opinion, upon learning that in addition to years of happy gardening memories Bennett Weissman had left Marcia Larsen more tangible assets, including the sum of nearly half a million dollars. And at least one person had known very well that he was leaving it to her.

* * *

"Of course I'm sure, don't you think my father ever talked to me? You don't dispossess your kid of a half million dollars without at least mentioning it. Or you don't if you're the kind of man my father was. He said she'd get the money if anything ever happened to him, and would I please just expect it and not try to cut her out of anything, because he wanted her taken care of comfortably. That was the word he used, *comfortably*. My mother would just have died, of course. She thinks comfort is so un-chic."

Mona Weissman had apparently decided that good grooming was un-chic. The little-girl look of yesterday had vanished; today her short mouse-colored hair was held sloppily back by four bobby pins and a rubber band. Instead of her neat skirt and blouse she wore a man's too-large blue shirt, tattered dungarees long past their wash date, and a pair of canvas sneakers.

"You mean," probed Edwina, "you knew, but your mother didn't." Which made sense; the idea of Serina Weissman giving up half a million dollars without a fight was just too foolish to be considered.

Mona scowled, shifting loutishly, scratching at her scalp with a grimy, bitten fingernail. Without asking she lit up a cigarette, glanced about for an ashtray, and tossed the match into the wastebasket. It all made Edwina regret intensely that she had ever felt sorry for the girl, even for one minute.

"I didn't tell her," Mona said, "she'd have squashed Marcia Larsen like a bug. Besides, my father was happy for once." She shot Edwina an insolent stare. "I guess you wonder about me."

Mona had apparently absorbed her personality—at least, the one she had chosen to use today—along with her costume, from some bowdlerized, poorly understood version of Kerouac's *On the Road* or possibly from Brando's *On the Waterfront*.

Either way, a dose of reality was in order.

"You overestimate yourself and underestimate my curiosity," Edwina replied, watching the girl drop ashes onto the rug. It was an old red Tabriz, rescued by Edwina from her father's study shortly after his death; calmly she imagined rolling Mona into some less venerable bit of floor covering and dropping the parcel, suitably bound and weighted, into Long Island Sound. "What I'm wondering, actually, is how you're going to pay me."

She named her standard daily fee minus expenses and took an unregenerate pleasure in watching Mona straighten with the shock.

"You're kidding," the girl said flatly.

"Not at all. Are you? Or is this all really just an angry gesture at mommy dearest? Talk to me, Mona. The clock is running and your presentation isn't measuring up to yesterday's. If your father were here, I doubt he'd be impressed."

Mona's face crumpled like a sodden Kleenex. "Don't you dare talk to me about my father. Don't you ever dare." She began to sob in earnest.

Edwina sighed, thinking that McIntyre was right: She should get a real office and stop letting clients come into her home. It was going to take forever to get the smoke smell out of here. Had she fancied the idea of plasterboard cubicles, there were any number of buildings full of them for sale; while Mona wept, Edwina considered buying one, deciding again to wait while prices fell even more. Never buy on a downtick, her father had always said, and as at his death he had owned most of Litchfield County, she regarded his advice as reliable.

Digging an ashtray from a desk drawer, she pushed it at Mona. "You could always go to the police."

Pouting, the girl stubbed out her cigarette. "I did, but they don't believe me. They say all the evidence is for suicide. Something about grit on his hand, and no marks on him except the gunshot wound, and no fingerprints of anyone but him."

Embedded gunpowder grains, Edwina realized, were evidence that the victim had fired the weapon. Interesting that the scene team had been so thorough; she couldn't help wondering why they had been. "What else did they do besides taking fingerprints?"

Mona frowned, thinking. "They picked up bits of things from inside the car and put them into baggies," she said. "They took pictures. And they took the bottle they said he'd been drinking from, which is also ridiculous if you ask me. More than a glass of wine and my father got the giggles. He never drank so much as they said he had that night. He'd have gotten sick first."

She shook her head. "That bourbon had been in

the liquor cabinet for years. And the hat, well, you can't understand about the hat. But he was unbelievably attached to it. An ordinary gray fedora, he never went anywhere without it. He'd as soon go out without pants. But it wasn't there, not anywhere. I looked absolutely everywhere for it."

"Did you know your father was seriously ill?" They could get around to the money questions again later, Edwina thought—the questions about what Marcia Larsen would get and about what Edwina herself, she could already tell, probably wouldn't.

"No." Mona looked taken aback. "You mean . . . sick enough so he might die?"

At Edwina's nod she sat up excitedly. "Well, that explains it. That explains what I found in his closet."

She leaned across the desk in earnest. "You see, it was the funeral director. He wanted a suit of clothes for my father, and my mother refused to go in there, she's such a princess, she says I'm incapable but really she's the one. So naturally I had to get the things. It's what makes it all so crazy, don't you see, because if he was going to kill himself, only he wasn't going to kill himself, I'm sure of that, but if he *was* going to—"

"Mona. Wait a minute." Whatever it was, thinking of it had cleared this girl's switches; her sullen pose had dissolved utterly.

"—then he wouldn't have had to do it with a gun, and not exhaust fumes, I mean, really, that must be a terrible way to—"

"*Mona.*" She slammed the flat of her hand onto the desk; the girl blinked in startlement. "What was it? What did you find in your father's closet?"

"Oh, right. I didn't tell you about that part yet, did I?" Mona shrugged. "Well, he was a doctor, you know."

"Yes, I do believe we have managed to establish that fact," Edwina said, thinking that sometime in her life she had apparently done something, or perhaps was only going to do something, very wrong and wicked indeed, and this girl was her cosmic punishment.

"So of course he could get any kind of medicine he wanted," Mona continued inexorably. "Like if he wanted a sleeping pill he could get a sleeping pill, or if he wanted a—"

"Mona." Edwina clasped her hands together so as to avoid putting them around the girl's neck. "You found precisely what?"

Mona's eyes widened. She tipped her head. The effect was of being peered at by some small dithering owl.

"Well, that's what I'm trying to tell you if you'd let me. Of course I'm not exactly sure, that's one of the main problems of him being dead is that I can't go and ask him. But there's a little IV pole in there, the kind with wheels, and some plastic IV bags of fluids, and some vials and syringes."

Uh-oh. "What does it say on the labels of the vials?"

"Some say morphine, and some say potassium. And there was a gadget with IV tubings and two clear cylinders, and the tubes have little plastic wheels on them. I think that's called a—"

"Piggyback," Edwina supplied. "For running medications in without mixing them together. The cylinders are volutrols, and when the first one empties the second turns on automatically, so you don't have to keep fiddling with them all the time."

"Right," said Mona. "And I can understand if he was sick and thought he might die, because he'd always said he didn't want to die in the hospital. He was funny that way, he always thought hospitals were really good for other people but never for himself."

She took a breath. "But it's also why I don't believe he shot himself at all, I mean, it makes absolutely no sense to me, does it to you? Because why would he do it that way when right there in his closet he had—"

"A device with which to commit suicide," said Edwina. "If you're describing it accurately, and I think you probably are, then it sounds to me as if your father built himself a gadget to use in case he got so ill that he decided to kill himself."

It was simple: You set it to run in the morphine, and that would put you out. Once you *were* out, it switched over and ran in the potassium. And the potassium put you out forever.

"Yes," said Mona. "So what I want to know is . . ."

She bit her lip; her voice when she spoke again was wavery. "If my father did kill himself, it would be all right with me. I mean, if he thought it was for the best, I would try to accept that. He had a right to make his own decision. People should be able to make their own decisions, don't you think so?"

Her face stiffened into a small white mask of hate. "But that's not what happened, Miss Crusoe. Someone murdered him, and I'm going to find out who it was." She got up from her chair.

"So I guess it's up to you," she said, "whether you help me or whether you don't. I won't have any money until my father's will finishes probate and even then my mother might get her hands on it. She's very good at that. I wish poor Mrs. Larsen luck."

She paused at the door. "Either way, though," she promised, "I am going to find out who stole my father's chance to use his own suicide machine."

FOUR

"MARTIN, why did the scene team go to all that trouble over an obvious suicide? I mean, when a man runs exhaust fumes into the passenger compartment of his car, then sits in the front seat and shoots himself through the head—well, it's pretty clear to me that he meant to accomplish something fairly serious."

McIntyre looked up from the dining room table, where he had opened his portable typewriter amid a clutter of his evening's paperwork. "Because," he replied, "I've told them if they ever don't, I'll be forced to have their heads stuffed and mounted, hang 'em like hunting trophies in the squad room as an example of what happens to guys who screw up. Or," he added, "girls who do."

"Oh," said Edwina. "You mean because it might look like one thing at first, but later . . ."

"Exactly. Only by that time the evidence is trashed, unless you got to it the right way in the first place." He frowned at a sketch he had withdrawn from a folder of reports, transcripts, and other departmental forms. "You can't know for sure what happened, so you find out." He riffled through the folder again.

"By," he finished in what was for McIntyre a most irritated tone of voice indeed, "some sort of halfway decent investigative procedure. Which has not been employed here," he slapped the folder shut, "unless this is supposed to be a rough first sketch of that Beers Street location and someone downtown is still busy playing Rembrandt with the final one."

With an effort, Edwina restrained herself. She would have loved hearing more about the Fellowes case. All she knew so far was that this morning's fire had at last been extinguished, the prisoners all unharmed and farmed out on an emergency basis to various other jails and correctional institutes, and that despite his apparent escape attempt Craig Fellowes remained in custody.

But McIntyre clearly was not in a mood for questioning, and the situation was otherwise so idyllic that she could not bear to spoil it; not often did they manage to spend an evening at home together, even if they were both contemplating bloody murder.

Sinking back onto the sofa, she propped her feet up on her father's old burgundy leather hassock, a childhood icon imported from the Crusoe estate in Litchfield. In the kitchen waited a cold lobster salad with seedless green grapes dressed in McIntyre's homemade mustard mayonnaise, along with a loaf of garlic French bread and a bottle of chilled Chablis.

The shiny little stainless-steel espresso maker McIntyre had given her for her thirty-seventh birthday hunkered on the counter, eager for its chance to whistle out aromatic puffs of steam; the stereo was playing Rudy Van Gelder's "Lush Life" with Ornette Coleman on trumpet, while in the apartment's long windows spread a sunset so red that it barely looked decent, much less natural.

Savoring a sip of an ice-cold martini along with a recurrent sense of her own good fortune, Edwina returned tranquilly to the page of questions she was listing for herself.

Why, she printed, would Marcia Larsen not tell me about the money Bennett Weissman left her? Why would Weissman plan to kill himself one way, then do it in another? And who *didn't* know about his suicide machine?

Amidst such questions, she always found the apartment around her to be like an oasis, filled as it was with her own familiar things reassuringly arranged in their own places. Upon the antique spruce and teakwood chess table stood the ivory chess warriors brought back by her grandfather Crusoe from one of his China trips. On the hearth the andirons gleamed with fresh polish; the parquet floors glimmered and the Turkish carpets glowed, recently restored to jewel-like splendor by Mr. Ziyadeh, the rug merchant.

Over it all from the mantel gazed the oil portrait

of her father, E. R. Crusoe. Shifting in Edwina's lap, Maxie made an unhappy face at the painting, as if fearing the image of the serious old gentleman might break its long silence. But this was only a little less likely now than when E. R. was alive; as diplomat, industrialist, and smoother of the way for presidents from Roosevelt through Kennedy and beyond, E. R. Crusoe had always been the quiet type, having enthusiasm more for plain deeds than fancy phrases.

"So once the scene investigators had gone into things," Edwina said to McIntyre, "they decided it was suicide. Weissman's death, I mean, so their report went along with the body to the coroner, who performed the autopsy and made another report ruling suicide officially, and that ended it. Is that the way it goes?"

McIntyre continued studying the Beers Street sketch, turning it first one way and then the other. "That's the way," he agreed distractedly. "It was the cadaveric spasm that clinched it."

Edwina sat up straight. "Cadaveric what?"

"Spasm," he repeated. "Weissman's hand was clenched on the pistol grip. You can't get a gun stuck into a dead person's hand that tightly. It's the nervous system shock, happens sometimes when people shoot themselves. But not when other people shoot them," he finished, "which is the important point."

"Martin, why didn't you tell me about this before?"

He looked up. "What? Oh, hell. I'm sorry, Edwina, but I just heard about it in passing today and my mind is full of . . ."

He motioned at the papers before him. "This guy. He must have hidden matches on him somehow, but how he got a fire that size started without anyone noticing is more than I can figure. And how he lured women into a basement. . . . Any sane person would as soon cuddle up with a pit viper as go anywhere with him."

Edwina considered this. "Maybe they weren't sane persons. There are lots of women on the streets. And going somewhere alone with a stranger who offers you ten dollars is not exactly a testimonial to a person's mental balance, but they do it."

McIntyre shrugged. "I guess. Anyway, talk to the techs and they'll say they don't care if Bennett Weissman had an atomic bomb in his closet. Bang, he shot himself, case closed. There's not a speck of anything to show otherwise, and plenty says he did."

"Except the hat. What do you suppose happened to the hat?" She put aside her sheet of questions as McIntyre got up from the table, stretched, and began clearing away his own paperwork.

"Don't know," he replied, grimacing at the typewriter as he closed but did not latch it.

Seeing this, she began making solitary after-dinner plans—a long soak with bath salts and the new Penguin edition of *Pride and Prejudice* that she had been meaning to treat herself to—since if McIntyre had not finished what he meant to write now, he would surely be hunt-and-pecking at it later.

"Maybe," he added, "he lost it. Maybe that's why he killed himself—couldn't live without his hat."

"Martin, it's not funny." In the kitchen she took the salad from the refrigerator and stood at the counter giving it a final toss while Maxie twined purringly around her ankles.

"Right." He popped the cork on the wine bottle. "Guy's got a dragon for a wife, a daughter who has a date on her carton that is what you might call expired, a bone disease with a three-in-ten chance of beating him, and a girlfriend with all the thrilling charms of Margaret Thatcher who's pushing resort hotel brochures at him. On top of all that, the poor guy loses his hat."

He poured the wine. "Hey, I'd shoot myself, too."

She stuck her tongue out at him. "You would not. For one thing, you don't wear a hat. And you don't have any girlfriend, either. Do you?"

He slung an arm companionably around her, raised his glass. "Of course I do, Edwina, you're my girlfriend. I mean, just because you gave in and married me doesn't mean you have to give up your hobbies. Many of which," he added, "I do so enjoy."

"You smell good," she said into his shirt collar.

He chuckled as the telephone rang. "Don't answer it."

"Not a chance."

Unfortunately, however, the volume on the answering machine was turned all the way up, so that when the instrument ceased its shrilling Harry Lemon's unhappy voice came through clearly.

"Edwina," Harry said, "I thought I'd better just call and let you know, since you said you were going to Weissman's office and I'm not sure you ever—what?"

His voice moved away from the telephone. "Oh, all right," he told someone impatiently, "I'll be right there. Tell them to put some pressure on it, for heaven's sake, that'll stop it. Doesn't anyone around here remember their first aid?"

Then he came back. "Marcia Larsen is dead," he said. "Shot half an hour ago in Weissman's office. I thought you'd want to know. Sorry to be the bearer of bad tidings. That's it." He hung up; the machine whirred and clicked its way back to "Answer."

"I suppose I could be wrong," said Edwina slowly, taking a tiny regretful sip of her wine. "But I think that swishing sound you hear is the Weissman suicide theory, circling the drain."

Marcia Larsen lay covered to the neck on a gurney in the major-trauma room of Chelsea Memorial Hospital's emergency department. The clutter of torn-open instrument trays, bloodied gauze, emptied glass ampules, and EKG paper strewn about the room testified to the frantic efforts that had been made to save her life. The stillness beneath the sheet testified to the failure of those efforts.

"I was down here admitting one of my own customers," Harry Lemon said, "when I heard them call a trauma code for the clinic building. By the time they got her into the room she'd lost most of her blood volume. The surgical team opened her up right there on the stretcher but they didn't have much to work with. Gunshot wound, severed everything major. They pumped up the shock pants and poured in volume but they never did get any pressure on her."

Marcia Larsen's gray eyes gazed blankly at the green-tiled ceiling. A brownish fleck of dried blood clung to her cheek. The skin of her eyelids was cool as Edwina gently closed them, wondering who would take care of the secretary's garden now that she was dead.

"I suppose," Harry said, "some intruder got into the clinics looking for drugs. The code team said the office was a shambles. The secretary was working late, must have left the door open while she stepped out, then came back and surprised him."

"Maybe," said Edwina, remembering the new lock on Weissman's door. "This happened when, around six?"

Harry nodded, and they moved out into the hall as a housekeeper came in to begin cleaning up the mess. The housekeeper glanced at the body, crossed herself quickly, and crouched to gather up the yards and yards of EKG paper that had spewed onto the floor during the resuscitation attempt. Behind her came nurses with a shroud kit, towels, and washcloths, and a basin of soapy water with which to ready the body for transport to the morgue.

In the hall a dozen patients with minor surgical emergencies sat or stood around nervously, waiting to have lacerations examined and stitched. One young fellow had sliced a three-inch gash into the flat of his palm. Another's big toenail had been torn from the nailbed and stuck up messily at the angle of an open trapdoor. A third man wore only an undershirt and boxer shorts, and held a reddened ice bag to the side of his head. When he lowered it to examine it anxiously, Edwina saw that half his ear was gone.

"She bit me," the man kept muttering in shocked, aggrieved tones, "I can't believe she bit me."

Edwina could; his knuckles were bruised and bloodied. "Why would anyone look for drugs in a journal office?" she asked, following Harry to the medical side of the emergency room. The patient population here consisted mostly of minorities and poor people: a very old woman with a neglected-looking bandage on her foot. A girl barely into puberty, jouncing a wailing two-year-old on her skinny knee. A sleeping man whose infected arm was so swollen that it appeared inflated.

"Do you want to know," said Harry, following her gaze, "why these people are here?" Ignoring the question she had asked, he thumbed through a pile of big manila envelopes, found the one he was looking for, and yanked two X-ray films from it. Slapping the films onto the light-board, he snapped on the illuminator and sighed as he scrutinized them. Edwina already knew what he was about to tell her, but decided to let him blow off steam.

"Because," he said, yanking the films down, "there is no one left to take care of sick or injured people in this city, unless they also happen to have money, except us."

He slid the films back into the envelope. "Send my patient back down for another lateral view, please," he said to the clerk behind the desk, "and ask them as a personal favor to me please not to overexpose it this time. This is diagnostic radiology we want here, not tumor obliteration."

"And," he went on to Edwina, "in the inner city, at least, being sick and having money are mutually exclusive conditions."

He parted the curtains of one of the cubicles that lined the medical treatment area. "Sorry, Ted," he told the patient within, "but I need one more chest X ray before I can send you home."

Edwina glimpsed a thin hand beckoning Harry, heard a harsh pleading whisper from inside the cubicle. Moments later Harry emerged, looking furious. "Forget that X ray," he called to the clerk, "and see if you can find me a bed on the seventh floor, will you? I'm admitting my guy with a pneumonia."

He turned to Edwina. "But," he went on, "private docs don't want Medicaid patients because they lose money on them, the fees the government will pay don't cover treatment costs. So the sick people put off getting treatment until they're so sick they can't wait anymore and then they come to the emergency rooms, which are obliged by law to treat them. At which point of course they're ten times sicker than they were in the first place, so the hospital loses ten times the money trying to fix them up again."

He looked grimly out over the waiting area. "It's a dumping ground, that's all. A dumping ground for sick poor people. And the people who make the laws still have fat-cat jobs and fat-cat health insurance benefits, so it's going to stay that way until the hospitals start going under. And then do you know who'll get blamed?"

He swung back to the admitting counter. "Doctors, that's who. Because doctors don't want happening to them what's already happening to emergency rooms—involuntary civil servitude, at an absolutely horrendous loss."

He slapped open his patient's chart, began scribbling an admitting note into it. "So from now on," he grated out, "guys like my buddy over here," he jerked his head at the curtained cubicle, "are coming inside. I'm just bringing them inside."

Edwina blinked, still wondering why a drug addict would search for drugs in what was obviously not a patient treatment area. "You mean he hasn't got pneumonia?"

Harry shook his head, still scribbling. "He has now. I've diagnosed him. Doctors are still allowed to do that, I hear."

"But Harry, if you give him the bed then somebody who really needs it won't be able to get admitted to the—"

Harry slapped the chart shut. "So sue me. Everybody else is suing me, what's one more? The thing is, he's HIV positive, he's got AIDS, and he's on AZT. As a result of which, due to the remarkably enlightened attitudes which persist about his disease, he's lost his job, his car, his house, and many of the people he used to think were his friends. Oh, and his health insurance, so he can't get a home-care aide and there's certainly no one in his rooming house to take care of him. I can admit him now and head off a crisis, or wait till he's so sick he *deserves* the bed."

Harry made a face. "So I'm admitting him. If the system's screwed up, it can be screwed up on behalf of my patients." He tossed the chart back onto the counter and glanced at his watch. "And now if you'll excuse me I have sick people to take care of."

Abruptly his expression softened. "Sorry, Edwina. I didn't mean to lecture you. I've been told I'm getting quite personally intolerable lately, what with the lawsuit and my caseload and all. And all the sick people." He shrugged contritely.

She smiled, thinking that if anyone deserved the chance to throw a tantrum occasionally it was Harry. "Incorrigible, yes; intolerable, no," she said, patting his arm. "Go on," she told him, "go stomp out some more diseases before they get too rowdy."

He brightened at the prospect—and, she realized, at the kind words, for Harry spent so much of his time looking out for other people, he had forgotten how to let other people look out for him;

at the pat on the arm he had actually seemed startled.

She would, she decided, call a lawyer for him herself.

But first she would examine a murder scene.

"Edwina," said the security officer posted at the top of the clinic building staircase. He was a tall, broad-shouldered black man in a blue uniform with a white shirt and tie, carrying a walkie-talkie in one hand and small notebook in the other. She had known him since she was a student nurse and he was a buildings and grounds laborer, fifteen years and many promotions ago.

"Mike," she greeted him. "Are the police still there?" She angled her head down the echoingly empty hallway, toward Bennett Weissman's office.

He shook his head. "They finished up a little bit ago. What are you doing here? I thought you quit the hospital, got to be a lawyer or something like that." He tucked the walkie-talkie in his pocket and stuck out his hand; she pressed it warmly.

"Not a lawyer. I do private consulting work these days, for people who have medical problems. You know, if they think they might be getting ripped off by a quack, or by some unscrupulous nursing home operator. I find out what the real situation is for them, cut through the medical jargon if there is any."

It was not a completely accurate description of what she did. But Mike had never needed accurate descriptions to make accurate assessments; his dark eyes appraised her easily.

"Bet you've got a whole lot of business," he said. "Half these doctors, they bother talking to you, you can't understand what they're talking about. Need a translator."

She laughed. "Yes, but most of them don't know any better, you know, if it won't fit on a history-and-progress sheet they've forgotten how to deal with it. It's when somebody starts flim-flamming people on purpose that I get involved. Mike," she laid it out directly, "can I have a look at the Weissman office?"

"Oh my." He shook his head. "Edwina, no-body's supposed to go down there without an of-ficial reason. I'm here taking names of anybody even walks down to their own offices, who they are, why they're here, what time it is, any ID they're carrying. This is bad, you know, and bad publicity."

He looked sorrowful. "I'm really sorry, Ed-wina."

Not for the first time, Edwina thought that if she needed anything watched, guarded, or pro-tected, she would want Mike Rosewater doing it, especially if the something were herself. He was big, but more than that he was smart, hard-headed, and utterly singleminded.

"Don't worry about it, Mike, I understand. It's just that I was talking to her this morning, the secretary who was shot, about Dr. Weissman, who supposedly killed himself?"

Mike Rosewater's dark face remained impassive. His regular gym workouts hardly showed beneath the custom-tailored uniform.

"I know who you mean. But I didn't know there was any supposedly. That come under the category of private consulting?"

"It didn't," she admitted. "Or at least it didn't for sure. But now that somebody's killed the secretary, well, I just don't buy the idea of some crackhead kid sneaking in here to look for drugs. In fact, with your guys on the job I don't buy the theory of a crackhead kid getting in here at all. Do you?"

"Be hard to do," he agreed. "Doors all locked after five. Somebody could hide, wait for everybody to leave, but my fellows stroll through pretty regular. You don't know your way around or you don't look right, be hard for them not to catch you. I have to say, I'm wondering myself how it happened. This building's been safe."

She could see his professional pride was wounded. "Unless," she suggested, "it was someone who belonged here, someone none of the guards would look at twice. Do many people work late in this building on a regular basis?"

That was what Marcia Larsen had been doing, although Edwina could not think of any reason for her to be doing it. With the new issue mailed and the next already in galleys it did not seem there could be much urgent work left, especially since Weissman was no longer there to generate routine tasks. But perhaps now that he was dead, the secretary simply had not wanted to go home.

"The detectives asked," said Rosewater.

"There's quite a few offices and some smaller labs in this building. Lot of the people who work in them don't keep regular hours. But they only have to sign in if they don't have ID and the door guard doesn't know them, and nobody has to sign to get out. So there's no real record. I guess the police mean to go around taking roll call."

Edwina didn't envy this portion of the cops' job, plodding from room to room asking the same questions, going back again to make sure they had talked with everyone, checking stories against one another. And coming up, probably, with nothing.

"In a way," she said, "I suppose it might be a good thing. If it turned out to be someone who belonged here, I mean, because that would mean the guards on duty hadn't missed any real obvious intruder."

Mike Rosewater looked down at her. "The cops won't see it like that. Even though those two worked together."

"No," she agreed, "they won't. They have to question all the people who might have seen something. But Bennett Weissman's death has been ruled a suicide, and unless something comes up to suggest otherwise they'll probably look at his secretary's murder as part of an attempted robbery, just a coincidental thing. It does happen," she said, unconvinced herself.

"The something that suggests otherwise maybe being you."

She shrugged. "Maybe. If I have any reason to

suggest it. But if I can't even get a look at the scene . . ."

She let her voice trail off discouragedly, which of course did not fool Mike Rosewater for a moment, as it had not been intended to.

"Edwina," he pronounced, "you know, I don't get the chance to visit with you often enough, our career paths being so dye-vergent in recent years an' all."

He gave these last words a sly twist; Mike Rosewater could not only pronounce divergent perfectly well, he could trace the word back to its Latin origins; in his spare time he played piano and Dixieland trombone, as well as a subtle, cut-throat game of bridge.

"Why don't you stroll along with me while I make sure everything's shipshape down the hall?" he invited. "I can keep an eye on the staircase while I check that Weissman's office is just the way the policemen left it, note that fact right down here in my book, you see, all very professional. And on the way you and I can chat about one thing and another."

It didn't look like a journal office anymore. It looked like a fair-sized tornado had touched down, flinging furniture and swirling drifts of paper as it went. On one wall was a single very clear handprint like a bloody slap; the rest of the room was similarly smeared, streaked, and spattered.

"Dear god," Edwina murmured, remembering

Marcia Larsen as she had been hours earlier: clean, proper, and well organized.

And frightened over something more than an affair with her boss. The contents of Weissman's will, perhaps? Now that Serina Weissman knew about it, Marcia Larsen's life was about to become unpleasant. Perhaps it was why she hadn't mentioned Weissman's legacy to her: putting off the inevitable, realizing Edwina would learn of it soon, anyway. Sufficient unto the day was the trouble thereof for Marcia Larsen—assuming she knew of Weissman's legacy herself.

Peering past the shambles of the secretary's chamber, Edwina saw Weissman's sanctum in the same condition: books yanked from their shelves, desk drawers dumped, and file contents scattered. Only the prized journal cover still hung straight, seeming now to gaze reproachfully down onto the mess.

"Someone had some time in here," she said to Rosewater, who nodded.

"Dinner hour," he agreed, "people who meant to go home'd be already gone. Ones who stay, they go get something to eat. She must have come back, surprised the guy."

"Still, it's strange nobody heard anything. Somebody had to have made some noise, tossing those chairs and turning Weissman's desk inside out. Didn't anybody even hear the shot?"

Rosewater nodded. "Guard was on his rounds, way down the other end of the corridor. He heard it, recognized what it was, radioed in, ran up here."

His look continued mournful. "Time he got here, people were starting to gather. Not many, though. Couple of grad students working in one of the labs, a doctor out of another one, they all thought it was some kind of explosion. One said it sounded like a high-pressure hose popping, the kind they use to run oxygen and medical gases from those big tanks they have in their labs."

Edwina frowned past the barrier of yellow crime-scene tape stretched across the open doorway. "So she was shot over there, fell or staggered toward the door, collapsed against this wall."

"Flung her hand up to catch herself," Rosewater agreed. He winced at the bloody print. On the floor below it, part of a white chalk outline was visible, most of it obscured by the corner of the desk.

"He tried to help her, the lab doc did," Rosewater went on, "but from what I hear she was on her way out by that time. When the stretcher got here she was already unconscious."

"No one heard her say anything about who did it?"

He shook his head. "I heard the cops asking the doctor. He was crouched right over her till the code crew arrived. He said she was just losing all kinds of blood too fast, couldn't really talk. She just rolled her eyes at him, he said."

Rosewater turned from the doorway. "He was pretty upset, the doc was. Not being able to help, and all the blood and all."

"Yes, I suppose," said Edwina distractedly.

The blood was upsetting, but more than that it was confusing, like a screen of grisly nonsense getting in the way of something sensible. "Did the police say anything about the position of the body? Anything odd about it, that you can see from the chalk outline?"

He turned back reluctantly; Edwina understood. The more you saw of this place, the worse it got. The little dish of paper clips from Marcia Larsen's desk was shattered; tiny glittering objects lay scattered across the green flat-pile carpet. Her glasses had fallen beneath a chair, the frame twisted and one of the lenses smashed. The amount of blood was the absolute worst thing, though, as if the more you looked at it the more of it there was.

Blood, Edwina reminded herself, is just the useful stuff the body pumps around. It's no more ghastly than gasoline.

But when the body stopped pumping it, it was.

"Behind the desk," Mike Rosewater said slowly. "From there to there. She was way over there in the first place."

"All the way," said Edwina, "inside the office. Considering the amount of disturbance you see before you, don't you find that just a little odd?"

"Uh-huh. Now that you mention it, I sure do. I didn't hear the cops say a thing about it, either. But you're right, some secretary all alone here working late finds a guy in the middle of tossing the place, she'd go get somebody."

He ran his gaze once more over the destruction. "When she got shot she was already ten, twelve steps in there. You could say she knew the guy, but by the mess he'd made she'd still have had to know something was wrong. Pretty bad wrong, too, I'd say."

"Unless it *was* just some kid," Edwina mused, "she didn't know he had a gun. Then I can see her confronting him."

She thought back to Marcia Larsen's schoolmarmish manner and to her comment about not being forceful enough. "Maybe," she added. "I don't suppose they found the weapon?"

"Nope. Funny place to be looking for drugs, too, don't you think so? And look here, one other thing."

She followed Rosewater's gesture. The devastation was shocking, but in addition there was something strange about it, something even more strange than a handprint in blood, a harmless woman's shattered eyeglasses.

Only, she couldn't quite put her finger on what.

"I don't know about you," Mike Rosewater said, "but when I go looking for something I look in the standard places first off. Places where I think what I'm looking for might be. You just run your eye over that room again, tell me what you see about it."

"All right. All the books are pulled off the bookshelves. The manuscript pages are scattered, the back issues of Weissman's journal are tossed around, the desk drawers are emptied . . ."

"Yeah. Now tell me the only real doctoring item you see in there. The thing looks like it might have doctor tools in it, or maybe even a supply of drugs.''

"Oh." She looked again. "Right, that little white ceramic table on wheels. In an old doctor's office, they'd have kept a tray of minor surgery instruments in the drawer, maybe some glass syringes and so on."

It was a pretty little object, dating she thought from the thirties or the forties. Just the sight of it conjured up images of nurses in starched uniforms and white caps, friendly family doctors with twinkly eyes, and a whole era of trust in medicine that seemed lately to have gone the way of the dinosaur. Now it lay tipped onto its face, the small vase of dahlias that had been on it smashed and scattered across the rug.

"But I don't—" she began, and stopped. "It really is the only clinical thing here, the only thing that looks medical."

"Uh-huh," Mike Rosewater said. "Looks like someone might keep drugs in it, doesn't it? Compared to all the other stuff, I mean. But look at the way it's lying there."

"On its face. On the drawer, with nothing around it but the flowers that were on top of it."

"Right," said Mike Rosewater. "Because nobody opened it. Whoever was supposed to be looking for drugs didn't look there, in the only place they ought to look."

"Interesting," Edwina agreed with him. "And I gather her purse was not stolen, money, credit cards? That sort of thing?"

He shook his head. As he did so another guard

reached the top of the staircase and called to him.

"Mike, like we needed more problems. Gonna hafta get some extra guys in, put 'em on the walkway and in the parking garage before the second shift lets out. I already locked up the street-level elevators in the garage building."

"How come?" Rosewater frowned as Edwina followed him back to the staircase. The new guard was younger, fresh-faced, and to her surprise was wearing a revolver beneath his blue uniform jacket.

"And why're you carrying?" Mike demanded of the guard. "You aren't supposed to have your personal weapon on the job, dammit, what the hell is going on around here? I haven't given anybody permission to—"

"That's the other thing I came to tell you, we got more cops down in the security office, also the president of the hospital corporation and a whole bunch of hospital lawyers. They say we all gotta carry until further notice, any guard who's checked out on a weapon and got a carry permit. Starting right now."

Rosewater's face darkened. "Oh, great, we're going to turn this place into an armed camp? Just what I need, a lot of paper pushers looking for some publicity, turn my department into *Dirty Harry*."

The young guard shook his head earnestly. "It's not that, Mike, it's the other one. The crazy guy . . ."

Noticing Edwina, he stopped. "Evening,

ma'am. Uh, Mike, maybe we better talk about this in a minute.''

"Spit it out," ordered Rosewater, "this lady isn't going to faint at whatever you've got to say."

"Uh, well, okay. Thing is, that crazy guy escaped. Couple hours ago, the cops say, only they didn't tell anybody right away 'cause they thought he might still be hiding in the jail. Only he wasn't, and they say he's real mad at the hospital, something about getting beat up with leather belts or something. I dunno, that doesn't sound right to me, but—"

"Restraints," Edwina said, "they'd have had him in leather restraints. He was acting psychotic."

Helplessly the younger guard waved a hand down the corridor. "They think he's here. I dunno, it all sounds pretty nuts to me, but—"

"He is nuts," Edwina put in, and Rosewater nodded.

"Yeah," the guard agreed, "that's true all right. And now they think he's maybe the one killed the secretary, like for a revenge kind of thing, you know? And now he's maybe hiding in the hospital somewhere, you know, waiting to do more."

"You mean," demanded a new voice, "Craig Fellowes is *here?*"

FIVE

THE young man in the hallway kept patting and smoothing his mat of dark, curly hair, which seemed somehow not to belong atop his small, nervously bobbing head. His voice, too, contradicted his looks: deep and resonant, it seemed produced by some trick of acoustics, for surely there was no room in that narrow chest for such enormous sound-making apparatus.

Nevertheless, the voice continued booming out, as bizarre as it was irritating, and the rest of the fellow at least was all of a piece: face round and pale as a pan of milk, hound-dog brown eyes peering weakly from behind wire-rimmed glasses, soft moist lips flapping ceaselessly in ill-tempered dismay. A plastic ID tag pinned crookedly to the pocket of his short-sleeved rayon shirt said his name was Vincent Perillo, M.D.

He planted himself before them, wringing his pale hands anxiously and goggling about with his glassy, faintly bug-eyed stare. "Here?" he shouted. "In the hospital complex? But this is outrageous, something must be done about it immediately. Don't you people realize important scientific work is going on here?"

He made it sound as if the predations of a murderer had been designed to thwart him, spitefully and without regard for his all-important tinkering with the obscure genetic machinations of this, the hitherto-unknown physiological implications of that.

Ignoring Edwina, he went on glaring at the two guards, each of whom he clearly considered his inferior intellectually and in every other way. The younger one went blank faced almost at once, but Edwina caught his dismissive lip twitch.

Perillo caught it, too. "Now you just look here," he began angrily, his fists clenching and his jaw thrust out.

The young guard blinked in pretended boredom, and pointedly did not pick up Vincent Perillo and drop him, squalling and flapping, over the stairwell's railing.

"Mike," he drawled, turning away. "Catch you later."

"Hey!" Perillo shouted, nearly dancing in his sudden rage. "Hey, you, you can't just walk away from me like—"

Mike Rosewater stepped in front of him. "Edwina, this is Dr. Perillo. He was first on the scene, and he tried to save the victim. Sorry it didn't work out, sir. I guess she was just too far gone. I'm sure it must have been upsetting for you."

Perillo drew himself up, placated by the "sir"

and by the mention of his rescue efforts. "Yes. Well. I'm afraid there's not much even a top-notch endocrinologist can do with a gunshot wound through the aorta. Poor woman." He planted his hands on his hips and frowned pettishly at Rosewater. "But I suppose none of us are safe around here these days, are we? Bad enough when we thought it was a robbery, now you've let a madman get into—"

Edwina stepped between them and introduced herself. Perillo regarded her offered handshake as if fearing some insult might be hidden in it. His grasp, when it closed unenthusiastically on her own, was as chilly and damp as a cuttlefish.

"Miss Crusoe is an investigator connected with the case," Mike Rosewater lied smoothly.

Perillo looked again at her, taking in her straight black denim skirt, white silk blouse, and silver earrings. She thought he also noticed her stockings and heels, and was glad at the moment that she had worn them; such trappings might be uncomfortable, but there was no sense letting people get any silly notions out of a carelessness in costume.

"Well," he sneered, "it's about time we got somebody besides the Keystone Kops to stick around," and of course Mike Rosewater did not backhand him down the stairs at this remark.

Top endocrinologist indeed, Edwina thought; funny how people wound up in the jobs they were suited for. Weird glandular ailments were the perfect specialty for this officious little twerp.

"But your police colleagues have already interviewed me," he added, "and I'm afraid I really don't have time to repeat all the information I gave them. Besides, instead of going over the same ground twice, I should think you'd be better off—"

"I'm not with the police department," Edwina said.

She offered her card; he snatched it and scowled at it. As he read, his expression grew outraged; she had known it would. "You mean to tell me you're just some nurse, snooping around here on your own?" he demanded.

Just some nurse. On your own. The idea of nurses doing anything on their own was still anathema to some physicians, but Edwina had not for some time met up with this backward notion in the unembarrassed flesh. She wondered whether he might be more impressed if she were to reach out and grasp his small pink nose, and give it the sharp vicious twist it so obviously was crying out for.

"Well," Perillo huffed, "we'll just see about this." With a quick angry motion he stuck the card into his shirt pocket, as if confiscating it. "I don't know what academic medicine is coming to, when physicians have to tolerate the brazen intrusions of—"

"I'm a private investigator," Edwina broke in, "and if you can spare another few moments from your important work I have a couple of questions I'd appreciate the chance to ask you."

"—trouble-making amateurs," Perillo went on

spluttering, "with no intellectual training or sense of propriety—"

"For instance," she continued, "I gather there are only offices on this corridor. Your lab must be around the corner, at the other end of the hallway?"

He looked even more peeved. "Yes. The other labs are all closed up now. And you," he aimed a finger at her, "are not supposed to be up here. The police—"

"But the others, technicians in the laboratories, were here when the incident occurred. How many, half a dozen or so?"

"About that," he snapped. "But—"

"Are their labs nearer the murder scene, or is yours?"

"Theirs are nearer. I'm having to make do temporarily with less space than I—wait a minute, what are you trying to say?" He took a step back, outraged.

"I'm not trying to say anything, Dr. Perillo," she replied mildly. "I'm wondering, that's all, how the person farthest from the incident happened also to be the first one on the scene."

Perillo's soft, moist mouth worked wordlessly.

"But I suppose," she continued, "the police must have asked you that. And as you haven't time to repeat what you told them, I'll simply have to ask them about it myself. Won't I?"

She turned. "Good talking to you, Mike. Give my regards to your family, won't you?" She started down the stairs.

Rosewater had opened his book and begun jotting notes in it, studiously not laughing at Perillo whose jaw continued sagging. She had reached the first landing and started down the second flight of stairs when his voice finally reached her.

"Wait! Damn it all—"

He pattered down the steps behind her. It was all she could do not to stick her foot out; possibly a good hard landing on his backside would jolt whatever this fellow was using for brains.

"Miss Crusoe, please forgive me, I was terribly rude. It's just that—"

She stopped. Vincent Perillo teetered on the step above her, grinning down into her face in a way he probably thought was ingratiating. "It's just that I was so upset. Being in the middle of a clinical crisis, and feeling helpless."

He let his hands fall to his sides, his grin fading as his voice dropped. "It's been a while since I've taken care of real human patients," he went on in tones so self-accusatory she half expected him to begin beating his breast. "I'd forgotten how hard it is to lose one."

Kind of hard on the patient, too, Edwina thought, wondering if Perillo might have botched something crucial in the first aid department. She watched his face trying on one look after another; finally he settled on woebegone.

"I'll always wonder," he mourned, clasping his hands, "if there was something else I could have done for that poor wounded woman."

He was lying. He didn't like it that she'd asked how he'd happened to reach the wounded woman first, and liked it even less that she'd threatened to mention this question to the police. Now he wanted to win her over.

Above them, footsteps approached the stairwell, paused, and moved away. Mike Rosewater, she thought, checking to make sure she didn't need any help with Doctor Doom here.

Fat chance, Mike, she thought as the footsteps faded and she resisted the malicious impulse to quiz Perillo on his resuscitation technique. He would be the type who in an emergency could be counted on to hop about excitedly and obstructively, making a fool of himself by shouting useless orders at anyone attempting to accomplish anything.

"Bennett, too, of course," he added. "It just won't be the same around here without him. Although there was nothing at all I *could* do for him, he never once confided in me. A good man, Bennett was, and an absolutely excellent journal editor."

Edwina thought that if given the choice between confiding her troubles to Perillo and shouting them down a rat hole, she would definitely choose the rat hole. His expression mutated again, this time into a shy smile.

"But you mentioned you needed information. Of course I'll be happy to help you in any way I can. Would you like some coffee? I just made a fresh pot, down in the lab."

He caught her hesitation, misinterpreted it. "Come now," he pleaded, "I've apologized for my rudeness. Don't hold it against me, I'm really very sorry."

He held out his soft moist hand; she managed not to see it, while regretting that she had never taken the time to learn jiujitsu. This fellow did so badly need a swift emphatic flipping.

"Apology accepted," she said, "and coffee sounds good."

"Wonderful," Perillo said. "I hope there's a clean cup. I'm afraid we scientists aren't nearly such demons for cleanliness as you nurses are. But then," he added, unable to resist a final jab, "I suppose we're all best at what we've been trained for, aren't we?"

Climbing the stairs behind him, Edwina ignored the barb—scientists think, nurses clean up—for the sake of the promise it held: Vincent Perillo was the kind of guy who just couldn't keep his mouth shut, couldn't resist a crack even though it would have served him a great deal better to keep silent. She had known quite a number of young men like him: every June the medical schools disgorged a new crop of them into hospital-based training programs. Usually the savage misery of internship beat most of the attitude out of them, occasionally even permanently.

But sometimes it didn't. Sometimes it only made them bitter and mean, the way abuse will turn a nippy mutt into a yard dog capable of taking a chunk out of you.

Without at all meaning to he'd already told her he was lying about something: the quick about-face in attitude, the anxious eyes and passive-aggressive body language, the sudden desire to win her over all said so. So she would visit his lab, which would smell like a mixture of cooking gas and rat droppings, and drink his coffee, which would taste like printer's ink.

And she would listen to him: to his insults, which he would be unable to stop delivering; to the self-congratulatory bombast, which apparently came as naturally to him as breathing; and to his lies, which he would try to disguise as conversation.

And when I've finished listening, she silently promised the man scurrying up the wide stairs ahead of her, I'll know what it is you're lying to me about—what it is, and why.

"I got there first," Perillo said, "because I ran. I knew it was a gunshot—I'm something of a pistol expert myself, actually, I do a little target shooting when I get a chance. There's nothing else quite like that sound."

He preened at his sharpshooter image of himself while Edwina cringed inwardly at the thought of Vinnie Perillo in possession of anything bigger than a cap gun. The laboratory facilities he'd somehow managed to secure were also more than he could handle, at least if their state of disorganization was any proof: heaps of unwashed glassware lay jumbled in the sink; unlabeled squirt bottles of chemicals littered the lab benches; ripped-open sacks of rat food and Vita-Mix spilled beige pellets onto the floor. All along one wall small white animals squeaked and scrambled frantically in their cages, their tiny eyes glittering and their claws making little pinging sounds on the stainless-steel wires that confined them.

The coffee was worse than printer's ink; more like battery acid, Edwina decided, as after a single sip she set her cup down. But she had been wrong about one thing: The lab didn't smell of rat droppings; it stank of them. The sawdust in the bottoms of the animals' cages was sodden, the stench an eye-watering assault.

As if suddenly noticing the mess, Perillo grabbed a rag and made a halfhearted swipe over the portion of lab bench nearest him. "Sorry things are cluttered in here. My tech's out and I've been working so hard, haven't even had a chance to let the cleaners in."

Several torn-out lab notebook pages drifted to the floor as he pushed the rag ineffectually about; grabbing them up he shoved them onto a pile of other pages. "In a few more days I'll have my final results, though, and then . . ."

And then the creatures would be probably sacrificed, having lived out their last days in filth, thirst, and hunger. Despite the spilled rat food littering the floor, there was none in their food pans.

"Perhaps as long as I'm here, I can give you a hand," Edwina said coldly. "The animals," she added, letting her fury edge her tone, "don't seem to have any water."

Without waiting for his permission, she crossed the filthy little room and seized two liters of sterile water from a dusty supply shelf. Flipping open the top of a wire cage, she plucked the bone-dry plastic water bottle out, filled it, and dropped it back into its plastic holder.

Sniffing the water, the rats crowded eagerly, squealing and biting one another for the chance to nuzzle desperately at the drinking tube. "Hey!" Perillo jumped up. "You can't—"

She turned with the second water bottle in her hand. If it were any bigger she might have brained him with it. "Tomorrow," she told him, "you are going to get a visit from the medical center's animal welfare committee. I know you are, because I am going to make certain that it happens. If you want to be ready, I suggest you provide fresh bedding for these wretched creatures, and a—"

Perillo looked stubborn, like a kid who'd been scolded for failing to clean up his room. "I'll deal with it," he insisted.

"Not good enough, Vinnie." She dropped a filled water bottle into the second cage; a second swarm of parched animals surrounded it. "You'd better get a bag for disposing of all this soiled bedding."

His face showed indecision, which heartened her: Maybe he wasn't the worst kind of spoiled rich kid after all. Money, she felt sure, was what had gotten him here. Vinnie definitely had that old-school-tie look, blurred now by too much junk food and not enough exercise, too much time under fluorescents. You could cheat your way through medical school—most didn't, but it was possible—and beat your way through training by a combination of shrewdness, stamina, and sheer bonehead stubbornness, but that did not get you lab space, grant approval, research funds. Not at Vinnie's age, especially; he could not, she judged, be more than thirty or so.

No, Vinnie had pull of some kind, and meanwhile his last name sounded familiar. Finally it struck her. "Are you by any chance one of the pharmacy Perillos?" The PRP label—Perillo and Reichert Pharmaceuticals—was found on well over a third of the prescription drugs in the hospital and on half the over-the-counter brands in most drugstores.

He nodded glumly. "Things got a little out of hand here is all," he said. Looking shamefaced, he glanced around the room, seeming to see it clearly for the first time. "I guess it is pretty bad, though. I get working and I stop noticing some things."

That was putting it mildly; still Edwina began feeling a twinge of unwilling sympathy for him. Probably he had never cleaned up after himself in his life, much less after dozens of lab rats. He moved to the first cage, slid the tray inexpertly from beneath it, nearly dropped the thing, and looked around helplessly. "You mind grabbing a trash bag? I think they're in that cabinet over there."

She fetched it; he dumped the tray and peered about for fresh bedding material, which was nowhere in sight. "Newspapers will do," she told him; a stack stood on the windowsill. Perillo handed her the tray and she began shredding strips of *Wall Street Journal* into it.

"Follow the market, do you, Vinnie?" She slid a fresh tray under a rat cage. The animals had finished drinking and were skittering about nervously, apparently in the hopes that humans giving water might portend humans giving food.

Perillo laughed self-consciously. "A little. Not much luck with it, though. My old man's the businessman in the family." He dug around in one of the open kibble bags and fished out a yellow plastic scoop.

"Better just give them a small amount. They look pretty famished," she told him. "Won't do your experimental results any good if the rest of your animals die of bloat. And scatter it around. If you put it all in one pile they'll kill one another getting at it."

Perillo opened his mouth to argue, thought better of it. "Oh. Yeah, I guess you're right." Carefully he dribbled pellets into each of the cages; the rats began gobbling them.

Leaving him to finish with the animals' care, Edwina dumped the coffeepot, started a fresh pot brewing, and began working with soap, hot water, and a pair of rubber gloves on the sinkful of glassware. A few minutes later Perillo dusted his hands in satisfaction. "There," he began, "I guess that's all that really needs—"

Turning from the sink, she grabbed a broom that was standing against the wall and thrust it at him. "Knock yourself out," she advised him, and after another rebellious moment he did.

Half an hour after that the room was transformed, glassware drying in wooden racks, the lab benches freshly wiped, clutter removed, and several bags of trash standing in the hall waiting for the morning pickup. In addition, the reek of neglected beasts had been replaced by the pleasant aroma of fresh hot coffee.

Vinnie's internal atmosphere had also changed considerably. "I, uh, really want to thank you for helping me out like this," he said. "Especially after I was so rude. I've been under a lot of strain lately is all."

In their cages the rats lolled in well-fed torpor. "What are you doing with them?" she asked. "What's the research you're working so hard on here?"

Thinking of what to say he patted nervously, automatically at his hair, which was when she realized it was not his hair at all. Under the lab's bright overhead lights, the too-sharp line of the hairpiece on his neck showed clearly.

"Hair," said Vinnie. "I'm growing hair on them."

It was past nine by the time Edwina telephoned McIntyre, waited while her call was routed through the communications desk at police headquarters on Canal Street, and received the message he had left for her: She was not under any circumstances to walk home alone; she was to let the desk man know she was leaving, then go to the front entrance drive of Chelsea Memorial Hospital, where a car would be waiting for her.

It was. "What'd you guys do to get busted down to driving inspectors' wives around?" she joked to the two uniforms in the front seat of the squad car as she let herself into the back.

The cop riding shotgun turned and grinned through the perp grill. "Hey, this is luxury duty. Most people we gotta drive anywhere don't smell near as good as you do, Mrs. McIntyre."

A flush crept up the back of his neck. "I mean, uh, geez, I hope that's not too personal a thing to say. Don't tell the inspector I said that, will ya? Geez, I gotta big mouth on me."

The cop behind the wheel glared sideways at his partner. "You gotta excuse my buddy here, Mrs. McIntyre, he don't know how to talk to nobody but creepos no more."

"Yeah, 'cause I spend half my time riding around with one," the first officer retorted. "Anyway, the inspector just called, he says you wanna meet him an' get dinner out? Or go home?"

"I get to pick?" She sat back against the vinyl as the car pulled smoothly from the half-circle drive onto York Street and headed downtown. Approaching the intersection of South Frontage Road, the squad continued slowly through the tunnel under the parking garage.

Here the glass fronts of a bookstore, a drugstore, and a Greek coffee shop reflected the sparse late-evening foot traffic: students headed home from the library, a ragged man pushing a shopping cart filled with his belongings, a gaggle of harmlessly roughhousing teenagers shouting to hear their voices echo from the concrete overhead.

"Hey, give that guy the hairy eyeball," said the

cop behind the wheel suddenly. "What's he doin' in that doorway? He ain't got no business there." He glanced in the mirror again as his partner observed the individual, who straightened under scrutiny.

"Evening, officers," the man called. "Everything all right?" He was tall and dark haired, in his early twenties, wearing faded Levis and a blue-striped polo shirt. Grinning lazily he stepped out of the shadows, approaching the squad with a confident air.

"Ah, he's okay," said the cop behind the wheel. The car pulled forward; the young man smiled after them for a moment, then turned toward the hospital buildings, tossing something into the air and catching it as he walked.

"Uh, guys?" Edwina said doubtfully, but when she looked out the squad's rear window the man was gone. She gave a mental shrug. It was one thing letting these guys drive her; trying to tell them how to do their job was something else again, and she felt sure neither of them would be as cheerful about it.

Besides, the fellow really did look perfectly all right, only a bit too . . . amused, or something. And what was that thing he was tossing?

Well, whatever it was, there was probably no law against it. Therefore, she asked the officers to take her downtown, which they liked because it was on their way to a just-received radio call to interview a car theft victim, and which she liked as it was on her way to dinner in one of her favorite restaurants, with perhaps a single dry martini for openers.

McIntyre was already seated in their regular booth when she entered the knotty pine–paneled dining room of the Lime House, a seventy-year-old New Haven landmark whose specialty was once bathtub gin but was now bathtub-sized martinis and food so wonderful it was fit to die for—which, considering the amount of cholesterol in it, one probably eventually would.

Before him was a plate of the fabulous little tidbits the Lime House served for appetizers: thin slices of salami rolled around cream cheese; star-shaped cutouts of goose liver pâté on bite-sized wheat crackers; whole boiled shrimps impaled on small wooden harpoons. The cherry tomatoes stuffed with lobster paste and topped with red caviar were Edwina's favorite.

Popping one into her mouth, she slid into the booth. A straight-up martini in a frosted glass appeared as if by magic, as did the waiter to deposit bread and butter and to inform her that Mr. McIntyre had ordered for both of them—sirloin, baked potato, and house salad.

"Getting confident, are you?" She smiled at him across the table.

He grinned back. "Figured if I didn't, you'd probably eat the tablecloth before the food had a chance to arrive. Besides, I have it on good authority: No man ever got divorced for feeding his wife rare sirloin, blue cheese dressing, and double-baked potatoes. I'm even," he confided, "thinking of having dessert."

She sipped her martini. "Keep it up, you'll make old-married-man status yet. How were things at the office?"

"Not good. Fellowes got out of the infirmary so easily it makes me wonder why we even bothered locking him in again. Bonked one of the male nurses, exchanged clothes and took the nurse's ID, laid the nurse on the bed all nice and peaceful, then rang to be let out. Guy at the desk takes a look at the screen, sees a nurse and a patient, hits the buzzer. Our man walks."

"You mean he just fooled them? Why didn't the desk officer see him hitting the nurse? And how *is* the nurse?"

McIntyre sighed. "Nurse's lucky. Embarrassed, got a killer headache. And the infirmary cells' cameras don't show the whole cell, we've been trying to get funding for that, but . . ."

But money for equipment was harder to come by than money for hiring actual live police officers, the city's budget being nearly nonexistent nowadays. What with the shrinking number of citizens paying taxes and the growing number consuming services, as a viable financial entity New Haven was rapidly becoming about as credible as a haunted house.

"Anyway," he said, "there's a little corner the camera can't see, right underneath it and about head high. Fellowes either knew that or figured it out. Afterward he waited for the split-shift duty to be coming in, flashed his ID at the door while there was plenty of distraction. It worked like a charm.''

He looked up. "So that's my little tale of woe. How about you?''

The food arrived: thick grilled sirloins and whole baked potatoes with fluffy golden mounds spilling out of them. Between bites, she described her own evening.

"I started out despising the idiot and wound up helping him," she said of Perillo. "Gad, what a klutz. For his sake, I hope he's as brilliant as he thinks he is and as rich as I'll bet he is, because otherwise . . ." She let the thought trail off.

"But you don't trust him."

She shook her head; her feelings about Perillo had changed, but she wasn't quite sure how. "It's not exactly that I don't trust him, it's just that he's so weird. He's got an answer for everything and it all makes sense, or sort of. I finally told him point-blank I thought he was lying to me about something, and he just said I'd misjudged him and he wasn't surprised, that his upbringing hadn't prepared him very well to deal with normal people. This was after I'd read him the riot act about his lab.''

She ate a bite of steak consideringly. "Really, Martin, you should have seen the dopey look in his eyes. I felt like some teenager's mother—as if he'd really wanted to clean the place up all along, but he didn't know how to, or maybe just didn't know how to get started.''

"So maybe he's not as despicable as you thought at first?''

"That's just it, I can't tell. If what he wanted was to make me feel sorry for him, he manipulated me beautifully. I hope I'm not getting so cynical I can't tell when someone's sincere. On top of which, he says he's trying to grow hair on bald rats, if you can imagine that without falling down laughing. Even more laughable, he's done it—or so he claims."

McIntyre speared an artichoke heart, chewed thoughtfully. "What's so funny about hair grower? He'll make a lot of money, and a lot of bald guys'll get him elected a saint if it turns out he's telling the truth."

"Right," she said, not glancing at his hairline. McIntyre was a good-looking man and he would go on being good-looking long after the thin spot at his crown met the receding patch on his forehead, a process she judged would be complete in about ten years, barring a medical miracle.

"But, Martin, the way he's doing it looks really fishy to me. I mean, I'm no research scientist, but if this guy'd grown as much hair on those rats as he says he has—they're very hairy rats, Martin, no patchiness or skimpy places—he ought to be further along in his publications. He says the coming issue of Bennett Weissman's journal is going to report his stuff, not as an article, but as an 'early communication.'"

"Get the jump, you mean?"

"Exactly." She tasted her double-baked potato, which was rich with cheese and butter: wild applause from her taste buds and pangs of guilt from her coronary arteries.

"In case someone else is working on the same thing," she went on, "it'll be on record that he got there first. That's not the only thing that bothers me, though. The other thing is, he's working alone with what looks like almost no equipment. It's as if he's barely being tolerated. Of course, considering what he's trying to do, it's no wonder. Finding a real honest-to-goodness hair grower is up there with locating the fountain of youth. Or like saying you're Napoleon."

McIntyre started on his own salad of white endive, radish bits, broccoli florets, and dime-sized circlets of Bermuda onion sliced thin enough to read a newspaper through, with a dressing of oil and dilled vinegar so light it almost wasn't there at all.

"And," she finished, "his lab rats were in horrible shape. I'm not sure his results, if he has any, are repeatable because of that. And if no one else can reproduce his work, then no one will accept any of the conclusions he's come to, even if they do turn out to be true."

"But Weissman's journal is Perillo's only clear connection with the Larsen woman. Previous to the shooting, that is."

"Right. Well, maybe right. But like Weissman himself, she is no longer available to discuss the matter. Or any matter."

"And you think somebody messed up Weissman's office to make it look as if robbery was the motive for killing her."

Edwina nodded vigorously. "There are a dozen small clinics in that building, Martin. Any one of them is more likely to have drugs. Well," she amended, "actually, they're not. Heavy drugs are stored in the pharmacy. But they look more like places where drugs would be kept, and a druggie would recognize that. I'm certain someone was after something else. I just think," she finished, "that someone should find out more about Perillo. He *was* the first one there, there *is* something odd about him, and I'm certain Marcia Larsen must have known the intruder. Otherwise, why go into the office? Why not just run?"

"Tell you what," he replied, "I'll find out who's on it, drop a word in someone's ear. Will that satisfy you?"

"Yes," she said gratefully, "it will, because I can't shake the feeling there's more going on there than meets the—"

McIntyre's beeper went off. "Damn. Just a sec." He slid from the booth and headed for the telephone alcove at the rear of the dining room, returning grim-faced moments later.

"Gotta go." He pulled some bills from his wallet, dropped them on the table. "Do me a favor and take a cab home, will you? I know, you've walked at night for years. But I'd just rather not have to think about you doing it until we get our guy back. So could you humor the husband?"

He tried to keep his tone light, but she knew him too well. "He did something, didn't he? Craig Fellowes just did something to someone."

"The uniforms that drove you over here," he answered as they left the Lime House, "they mention the call they were on?" The muggy night air was smothering after the air-conditioned comfort of the restaurant. McIntyre looked down the street for the squad that would be coming for him.

"Stolen car," she said, and he nodded, tight-lipped. "Why?"

"Because," he answered with a glance at his wristwatch, "it turns out the car had a guy passed out in the back seat, a buddy of the owner's. They were out drinking and the buddy got loaded, so his friends took him out to the car to sleep it off."

"Uh-oh. And where's the buddy now?" But she knew; missing buddies no matter how drunk were not Martin McIntyre's bailiwick.

"He's in an alley back of the Dwight Street housing project with his throat slit and all the clothes stripped off his body."

In the green and gold glow of the Lime House neon sign, his face was flat with anger. "Guy's wallet's gone, too. So's his middle finger."

Edwina's appreciation for the good dinner she had just eaten vanished abruptly and irrevocably. The black-and-white pulled up with its roof-rack beacons whirling. "So take a cab, please," he said, kissing her and striding toward the car.

"Martin? *Martin.* What *had* he been wearing? The guy they found, what was he—"

"What?" McIntyre spoke briefly to the uniform behind the wheel. "Blue-striped polo shirt and Levis. Why?"

"Because I saw him. Tall, dark-haired guy? Thin, long jaw, funny-looking smile?"

McIntyre nodded, listening carefully. Fellowes' picture had not been in the newspapers. "That's him."

She swung into the back seat as he got into the front. "He was wearing a striped shirt and Levis and he was heading straight for Chelsea. And—"

"Get on the radio," McIntyre said to the driver, "tell the desk to give them a call over there and let my guys know." He turned to face her through the grill. "What else?"

"He was smiling," she said. "As if he were looking forward to something, or was just . . . happy. I thought at the time he looked almost *too* happy. And he was tossing something up in the air and catching it as he walked."

"And?" prompted McIntyre. The officer behind the wheel glanced interestedly at her, too, as he spoke into his radio.

"It was small," she said, "and pale, like . . ."

Like a human finger.

SIX

THE clock on the glowing instrument panel of Edwina's Fiat convertible said 11:40 P.M. Twenty minutes earlier, having been dropped off in front of the apartment building and kissed good-bye by McIntyre, she had not gone upstairs—carefully, she had avoided saying that she would—but had hurried instead to her space in the building's parking lot. Firing up the little sports car, she had apologized mentally to her husband for the lie of omission, although perhaps it was not quite one: He had warned her against walking alone, not driving. Besides, he himself was not likely to return before morning, which meant he was unlikely to become worried about her.

Now with the Fiat's top down and the radio blasting a Mozart string quartet, she sped north on Interstate 91. A check of the phone book (the Fiat's vestigial back seat was useless for sitting but handy for storing basic snooping aids) showed that Marcia Larsen had lived in Cheshire, once a sleepy New England village but now a bedroom suburb quickly reachable by divided highway.

Increased accessibility had not done the town any good that Edwina could see as she sped down the exit ramp. The flat, loamy acres once given to truck farms and plant nurseries had succumbed to a real estate boom, sprouting fast-food joints, muffler repair outfits, and tracts of identical houses on identical quarter-acre bulldozed plots, from which the topsoil had been graded and sold off before development by the canny nurserymen and truck farmers.

But after a few turns the road changed to bumpier macadam, with ancient maples, clapboard Greek Revivals, and antique wooden saltboxes; only Marcia Larsen's red-brick cottage, the last dwelling on the dead-end lane, had been completed in the twentieth century.

Dousing the Fiat's headlights, Edwina let the car coast into the driveway, halting on the gravel before the garage. Probably the local police had not yet been notified of the secretary's death. Unless there was an alarm system or, god forbid, a dog, her own presence at this hour was unlikely to be noticed.

As it turned out, there was indeed a dog, but fortunately not one likely to raise any fuss. The shaggy English sheepdog peered expectantly at her through the vertical row of panes at the side of the front door frame, his pink tongue dangling comically from between his whiskered lips and his wriggles telegraphing welcome. None of the windowpanes displayed an alarm company's sticker, and the brass cylinder lock in the door yielded quickly to the small steel probe Edwina twisted in it.

Having before had urgent business inside locked places to which she lacked appropriate keys, she had several years earlier befriended a locksmith and purchased from him a dozen different locks, along with—after carefully persuading the locksmith—considerable practical tutelage in the art of picking them by twiddling at them with small metal tools resembling dental instruments.

The door swung open; the dog got up and danced in a joyful circle, toenails clicking on the red-tiled foyer floor. Then he raced down the darkened hall ahead of her, probably heading for the kitchen and the back door since by now he would not have been fed or walked for over eighteen hours.

A low table in the foyer held mail. Leafing through it by the moonlight streaming in the doorway, she found an electric bill, a circular advertising a Dog Daze Summer White Sale, and the bulletin of the Cheshire Congregational Church. Somewhere in the house a grandfather clock ticked hollowly. Out in the kitchen the dog paced, whining. There was a faint smell of lavender mingled with damp.

Closing the front door, she made her way down the hall toward the sound of the dog's anxious snuffling, located a light switch at last, and snapped it on. There was no reason not to do so and if by chance she were discovered here it would only look odder if she had not. The hall was carpeted in thick blue broadloom, as were the steps leading from it half a level up to the bedrooms. An arched opening to the living room gaped darkly; the clock was in there. Next came a pristine half-bath with guest towels and scented soap, and finally the kitchen—small, newly painted, and in good order. Seeing Edwina, the dog sat down and tipped his head.

One cup stood on the drainboard; one spoon lay in the sink. A fresh linen dish towel hung from a hook by the stove, upon which perched a red teakettle. From the breakfast alcove one could look out the window to the rear of the house; peering between the crisp white curtains, Edwina saw borders of dahlias neatly edged in angled bricks, lush geraniums in big clay pots, rosebushes espaliered to the back of the garage, and a stone birdbath whose circlet of smooth water reflected the moonlit sky.

The dog food was in the cabinet under the sink. She emptied a can of it into the animal's dish, freshened his water as he began wolfing the food, and tried not to think about his not ever seeing his mistress again. Perhaps someone would adopt him; she wondered where Marcia Larsen might have wanted him to go had she known she would be leaving him.

More than that, Edwina wondered what she was doing here and what, if anything, she ought to be looking for. From the moment she had known she would have the night to herself, she had known also that she would be coming—only not precisely why.

It did seem clear someone had wanted something in Bennett Weissman's office, and that whatever it was had probably not been found. Otherwise, the intruder would not still have been there searching for it when Marcia Larsen returned. Once she had interrupted the search, she might have been killed out of anger, for refusing to tell the location of the mysterious searched-for something, or simply to stop her from revealing the intruder's identity. But perhaps the something was not in the office at all. Perhaps it was here, instead.

The dog finished eating and went to the kitchen door, asking to go out. Noticing that the rear yard was fenced, Edwina let him into it; he seemed to expect this, so she thought it was what Marcia Larsen would have done. Not that it mattered, but being in her house made it seem so much as if the secretary were still alive, still concerned for her carefully mulched and watered dahlia beds.

Then the obvious struck: if someone had been hunting for something in Weissman's office, it was almost surely a thing of his being sought. And Marcia had said that he had a garden here, a patch of his own where he could dig to his heart's content.

In the garage among the well-kept gardening tools Edwina found a packet of slender bamboo stakes of the type used to prop up tall plants. One of these would do the job she had in mind; now, if only she could find the proper spot to do it.

But finding the proper spot proved not to be difficult. The moonlight turned the neatly mown lawn a blackish gray; against this the deeper black of the rich garden earth stood out sharply. Blue delphiniums and white nicotiana were luminous, while the fragrant pink rose blooms reflected a purplish hue as if some of the night sky's deep blue had seeped into them.

Weissman's plot was easily identifiable, for unlike Marcia Larsen, he favored orange and yellow pompon marigolds, multicolored cut-and-come-again zinnias, and low matlike ageratums with their massed clusters of fuzzy purple blooms: all flowers easier to grow than the more temperamental roses or dahlias, more befitting Weissman's amateur gardening abilities and likelier to reward him.

Into this plot of Weissman's Edwina began poking the stake, probing for something like a box or perhaps an envelope. Gentle pressure sent the implement deep into the soil; from it arose a clean, faintly mossy earthen fragrance. For a moment it occurred to her that she might enjoy living in a place like this, where one could have a real garden instead of pots out on a balcony. She had time to be surprised by the idea, for she had never found rural charms particularly charming when experienced for more than a single weekend, and then the end of the stake met a definite resistance, a sort of boggy half-yielding sensation that made her hand cringe reflexively for an instant from its grip on the implement.

Oh my, she thought, and sat down on the grass.

Alerted by this curious behavior the dog sat beside her, placing his big paw gravely and sympathetically on her knee. Absently she ruffled his shaggy head; with a soft whuff! he settled against her. The past few days, she thought unhappily, had been furnished with enough dead bodies already to populate a lifetime's worth of nightmares. Surely this could not be another one?

But it was, and after she had pushed aside enough of the rich garden earth to make sure of this, she took the dog with her back into the house. She would say Marcia Larsen had spoken of the dog, and that after the secretary's death she had remembered it and driven out to care for it. She would have to admit that she had picked the lock; this she supposed would cause her some measure of trouble.

Not dreadful trouble: the equivalent of a scolding. Likely she would have to surrender her burglar tools, as well, but the district attorney would be disinclined to do much more than that: It was an election year and thus a poor time to be prosecuting a homicide inspector's wife for carrying an illegal set of lock-picking implements about in her handbag, much less for breaking into the house of a murder victim with them.

No, it was the finding of the body that posed the difficulty. After a moment Edwina realized that the dog might have taken an odd interest in the gardening plot, and that she might have investigated it out of curiosity. Yes, this would serve; it was just barely possible enough.

Glancing at the animal she thought she saw an

expression of reproach in his eyes. He had indeed become interested in the body, whining anxiously as she uncovered more and more of it. But I didn't lead you, his look seemed to say; you led me.

"Sorry, dog," she said, patting him. Meanwhile, she had not come here to discover a body at all; from her bag she drew a pair of short white cotton dress gloves of the sort very proper ladies still wore to church. Conveniently, they were also the sort that improper ladies could use for searching houses they ought never to have entered in the first place, so as to avoid depositing their fingerprints in ways that would be too difficult to explain later. Pulling them on, Edwina began working her way through Marcia Larsen's kitchen and bathroom cabinets, her linen and clothes closets, and her bureau drawers.

Half an hour later she had found nothing of significance. If it ever had been there, perhaps whoever put a body into Marcia Larsen's garden had already taken it. Or perhaps it was in some difficult-to-search place, such as in the cellar behind a stone in the foundation. Sighing, Edwina looked at the dog, who looked back at her as if to say I told you so. She ruffled the dog's ears, glancing once more around Marcia Larsen's house and wishing she had been able to save the secretary somehow.

But there was no point to that, so she shut the dog into the kitchen, then went back out to the Fiat to phone Martin McIntyre on the cellular phone. Finally, intensely depressed and feeling certain she was overlooking something, Edwina summoned the police.

The woman buried in the earth of Marcia Larsen's garden was about twenty-five years old, brown haired, and a bit on the heavy side, wearing a cotton tank top, canvas shorts, and jogging shoes. According to the irritable medical examiner who had been gotten out of bed to scrutinize the body at the scene, she had been dead only a day or so. Cause of death, he opined sourly, was blunt head trauma.

The policeman who took Edwina's statement had no explanatory notions or theories, or if he had was not inclined to discuss them. What he was inclined to do was Mirandize, question, arrest, and confine her on a variety of relatively trivial but troublesome charges—trivial when compared with murder, at any rate—her possession and use of burglary tools being chief among these. Cheshire cops did not care for persons who picked their citizens' front door locks for any reason, even her story of an attempt at prevention of cruelty to animals being no excuse for this offense, in the officer's opinion.

The only thing that saved her from being canned immediately, as the officer chose to put it, was that he knew McIntyre, a happenstance for which Edwina thanked her lucky stars since as it turned out this policeman did not one bit care for New Haven's current political administration, most especially did not care for the law enforcement arm of it, and so would have been glad to stir up the sort of a scandal that might eventually get that administration—also as he chose to put it—bounced out on its butt.

"McIntyre," he repeated, softening slightly—about as much, Edwina thought, as the Rock of Gibraltar might soften in a century or so. "So he got married, did he? What do you know about that. I wouldn't have said McIntyre was the marrying type."

The policeman's name was Malley. Square-shouldered and heavy-set with thick sunburnt arms and close-clipped silver hair, he possessed bright blue skeptical eyes set into the face of an intelligent and extraordinarily tenacious bulldog. To Edwina's relief, the bulldog's jaws were not about to clamp down upon herself. Malley eyed the third finger of Edwina's left hand as if thinking Martin McIntyre's judgment must have slipped quite a bit since their academy days.

"Yeah, Martin was an all-right guy," he allowed grudgingly. A radio call had confirmed she was indeed married to him, as she claimed. "Helped me out once upon a time. You can go for now." He emphasized the final two words.

She hesitated. "What about the dog?" The excitement of so many strange people in the house had made him begin to bark and race about. Now he was shut in the garage, howling disconsolately.

"I gotta drop him off at the animal shelter," Malley said in disgust, "prob'ly he'll shed dog hairs all over my unit. Someone wants him in the next three days, they take him. Otherwise . . ."

He drew a stubby finger across his throat. The gesture made her furious.

"I'll take him," she said; Malley's salt-and-pepper eyebrows went up in surprise. "Until someone else claims him. Maybe one of Marcia's relatives will want him, or a friend of hers. I'm in the book if they want to call me about him."

Malley looked at her for a moment. His eyes still had that assessing, skeptical glint. "I guess you really didn't know her too well," he said at last.

They had already covered this topic. They had covered also her reason for carrying nutpicks, dental probes, tiny files, and an assortment of other small metal instruments, all tucked neatly in a folded chamois cloth and all swiftly confiscated by Malley.

"No," she said. "As I mentioned, I didn't. Why?"

He shrugged. "Lots of people new in town, even I don't know 'em, moved in from all over who knows where. But I knew Marcia Larsen, much as anybody knew her, I mean. Lived here in Cheshire all her life, like me. I even went to high school with her."

"And?" From the garage, the dog's howls came steadily.

Malley shook his head. "She was nineteen, the whole family went on a vacation trip. A reunion, like, with aunts and uncles, the whole bunch of 'em in three cars. A convoy, like, on their way to the Mount Washington Hotel. Eighteen-wheeler lost his brakes, wiped out the entire crew. All but Marcia. She walked away from it."

"Good lord. What about her husband's family?"

Malley shook his head. "Hated her. Feeling was mutual from what I heard. And no kids. After Larsen kicked off, she pretty much stuck to herself, which was nothing new. Never was a social type."

He looked around the room. "So what I'm saying, you'd best not be expecting anyone to come for the dog. Might want to just let me take care of it. Maybe easier that way."

Four technicians entered the house with a gurney; he aimed a thumb down the hall toward the kitchen and the backyard. There was no other way to get the gurney out there except by pulling a part of the garden wall down or jumping over it.

"I'll take the dog," Edwina repeated.

"Your funeral." He followed her to the garage.

The leash was red leather, dangling from a hook inside the door. Once it had been snapped to his collar, the sheepdog sat obediently as if accustomed to the walk routine, then trotted at heel to the Fiat and jumped in without having to be coaxed.

"Decent dog," Malley commented.

Edwina slammed the passenger side door and walked around the car.

"So," he went on as she slid behind the wheel, "the guys in New Haven think simple burglary went to robbery went to murder?"

She nodded. "That's what they did think." She

angled her head toward the house, where the technicians were coming out with the covered gurney. They hoisted the gurney one-two-three up to the level of the open ambulance. "I'd begun trying to convince them differently. This is sure to change their minds."

"And her boss, the doc, he shot himself last week." He made it a statement but his eyes had question marks in them.

She turned the ignition key; the Fiat's engine rumbled sweetly to life. "According to the coroner, he did."

"Uh-huh. And I'm the freakin' Dalai Lama."

She looked up at him in surprise. Behind him, across the street beneath the maples, a few neighbors in robes hastily drawn on over their nightclothes had gathered curiously; one of the onlookers separated from the group, his look suggesting he would get to the bottom of this nonsense right now.

"Officer?" He raised a curtly summoning index finger as if flagging down a taxicab. "Is there some trouble here, officer?"

Malley turned slowly, his gaze traveling up one side of the man and down the other. He looked across the street at the rest of the crowd.

"No," Malley said.

The man was wearing a cotton terry robe and rubber beach thongs. His gaze moved with childish expectancy from the house to the idling ambulance and back again. Hearing what Malley said, he frowned pettishly. "Look here, I'm a homeowner in this neighborhood, I just bought a house right down the road, here, and I have a right to know if—"

"You're a goddamn nosy ghoul," Malley said, "and I caught your boy with two of his friends behind the Safeway last night with a couple bottles of booze and some cherry bombs. Gave 'em all a good talking-to they won't forget, which if you'd try it once in while maybe I wouldn't have to so often. Any more questions?"

The man swung away and stalked back to the others. ". . . first thing tomorrow morning and complain," Edwina heard him saying as the group moved slowly off, the whirling roof-rack beacons of the departing ambulance strobing them with red.

"I thought you said you didn't know the new people," Edwina said as Malley returned his attention to her. The dog leapt into the Fiat's tiny back seat and lay down on it, whining.

"Exception," he said. "Some people, all you gotta do is get downwind of 'em one time. Anyway, about all this thing here . . ."

The ambulance pulled out, unblocking the driveway. Edwina shifted into reverse and waited with her foot on the Fiat's clutch pedal.

"You got anything more to tell me?" Malley asked, sounding genuinely curious.

"No. As I said, I only came out to check the dog."

And once the police investigation gets rolling, I'll be out of it entirely, she thought but did not add. After all, why would Mona Weissman need private help once the authorities started doing what she wanted done? She might be high-strung—that was a mild term, in fact, for what Mona Weissman was—but she wasn't stupid.

Malley nodded, unconvinced. "Yeah, well, I tell you what. I'm not gonna bust your tail for that kit fulla nutpicks you had, so maybe you could do me a favor, too. 'Cause, see, I liked Marcia. And your husband did me a good turn one time."

She looked up at him, prepared to thank him and to agree to some small reasonable request.

"You call me tomorrow," he went on before she could speak. "Write it on your calendar, so you don't happen to forget."

He leaned into the car. "And when you do call me," he went on, "you add in all the parts of the story you left out tonight, hear? You put every bit of it in there, 'cause if there's one thing I know for sure it's when I'm bein' lied to."

He straightened. "And lady, you are one crummy liar."

For a small-town cop, Malley was convincing in the authority department. A part of her actually enjoyed this; not often did she meet a person even faintly able to intimidate her. But most of her did not enjoy it at all.

"Why?" she asked. "If you're planning to make trouble for me, why not just start making it now?"

His answering look was scathing. "Ask McIntyre," was all he said.

McIntyre had in fact gotten home by the time Edwina returned to the apartment. But if he was concerned about the trouble his wife had been out somewhere getting into, he knew a good deal better than to mention it. Asking Edwina to keep out of trouble was like asking a fish to climb out of its aquarium and take up residence on a nice cozy sand dune somewhere.

Fortunately, to an experienced homicide cop like McIntyre, trouble meant bloodshed: past, present, or imminent. All other levels of difficulty earned from him at most the speculative lift of an eyebrow, accompanied by gentle inquiry as to how he might help.

This was just one of the many reasons she had consented to marry him, but it was the one for which she felt most grateful as, at half past two o'clock in the morning, she arrived at their apartment equipped with an English sheepdog pulling pantingly in eight directions at once, as well as with the rest of the story of the body in the perennial garden.

The dog he found enchanting, his face lighting boyishly as she entered with the animal. The story he did not like quite so much, and by the time she got to the part about Frank Malley his brows had begun their telltale elevation.

"Edwina," he said, ruffling the sheepdog's ears, "you have gotten your break-in kit confiscated by the only cop in the world who wouldn't drop you immediately and seriously into the clink for it. We're talking felony material here, dear."

Edwina sighed, once more struck by her own good fortune: He really was the most reasonable of men. Any other husband would be stomping about, waving his fists and demanding to know what the *hell* she thought she was doing, poking her nose in where it didn't belong and nearly getting herself arrested and possibly even murdered, and didn't she have *any* common sense at all?

Meanwhile she was also aware that she had come very near to embarrassing him seriously, a fact he also kindly forebore to mention, at least for the present moment.

"I do realize that, Martin, of course I do. But I couldn't very well say the door was open when I got there, could I? That would confuse the investigation, don't you think, if they thought someone else besides me could have been inside? And if I'd said I had a key I'd have had to explain how I got it, and produce it, too. Which of course I couldn't have—"

"And that," he agreed, "would have stirred things up even more. Good old Malley, you always could trust him to sort the crooks from the fools." At her indignant look, he grinned.

With an increased sense of having escaped, by the narrowest of hair's breadths, the sort of domestic uproar that had haunted her nightmares in the weeks between her acceptance of McIntyre's proposal and her actual pronouncing of the marriage vows, Edwina settled back into her chair with her iced glass of club soda.

"What did you do to make him such a fan of yours, anyway? Malley, I mean, at the academy?"

A shadow touched his face and vanished. "Long story," he replied lightly, getting up. "You suppose this dog would like to go out for a walk?"

Hearing the word *walk,* the sheepdog went instantly into ecstasies of wriggling, shivering anticipation.

"I think he'd like to run the Boston Marathon," she began; just then Maxie sauntered in, unaware of the shock awaiting him. The unexpected sight of the dog sent the black cat skittering, stiff legged and with neck hairs bristling.

"Wuff!" said the sheepdog brightly, dashing for Maxie.

"Meeyowrgloweryow!" retorted the cat, aiming an outraged swipe of his claws at the dog's nose.

"Yike!" cried the sheepdog, backpedaling madly, stunned at this harsh rejection of his friendliness. "Yike, yike, yike!"

Slipping on the polished hardwood, he careened sideways, slamming into a mahogany table upon which was perched an antique Chinese vase painted in chrysanthemums and dragonflies.

The vase teetered. Edwina lunged for it, tripping on the sheepdog's leash. Maxie sprang, claws extended, halfway up one sheer panel of the curtains; there he clung, swaying precariously and hurling down a variety of dark feline curses and imprecations.

"Mmp?" whimpered the sheepdog, hunkering in misery with his paws crossed on his nose.

"Mxlsprtzl!" spat Maxie as the curtains began shredding, lowering him slowly and inexorably to the floor.

"Blast," said McIntyre mildly, untangling the leash from around Edwina's ankles.

Edwina watched the mahogany table settle back on its four slim legs. The Chinese vase slowed its teetering and stopped. Reaching the floor Maxie dislodged his claws, muttered, and stalked purposefully toward the sheepdog. Martin made a grab for the leash while Edwina reached out and took the Chinese vase into her arms.

Then Maxie stopped, abruptly tiring of the contest. "Prutt," he stated, which apparently meant that upon consideration he supposed he might have been a little hasty.

At once the sheepdog began sniffing Maxie all over; this the cat tolerated with perfect patience, seeming to recognize that a capacity for instant forgiveness was rare in any creature's character, and not one to be disdained merely because the creature in question happened to be a—*shudder*—dog.

Carefully Edwina placed the vase on the mantel, out of reach of all but the most disastrous roughhousing. It had been bid upon, ardently and persistently, by museums in Boston, New York, London, and Los Angeles. Unfortunately for the bidders it had also stood for thirty years on Edwina's grandmother's kitchen table in the big house in Litchfield, where it had held forsythia in springtime, roses in summer, chrysanthemums in autumn, and holly boughs in winter.

Now Edwina traced a finger on the gold-painted pattern of a dragonfly, hovering eternally above a cluster of split-leaf palm.

Pattern, she thought, and turned to see McIntyre heading for the door, the dog lunging eagerly ahead of him.

"Back in a few minutes," he told her, smiling at the dog's antics. He was already in love with the creature; resignedly, she began planning cabinets within which family heirlooms might be safe. In the hall she heard McIntyre murmur to the animal, then the elevator doors opening and closing.

Pattern, she thought again: Weissman's apparent suicide, the ransacking of his office and the murder of his secretary, the body in Marcia Larsen's garden. Perhaps both Weissman and the secretary had been participants in the garden woman's murder, along with someone else. Then they might have been killed to ensure their silence, killed by the unknown third person.

The office ransack would have been for the evidence: something whose existence, perhaps, Bennett Weissman had revealed to the killer in an unwise attempt to get—or retain—the upper hand.

Glancing at the clock, Edwina thought she would run these ideas past McIntyre when he came in, and then close her eyes as soon as possible. After all, none of this was her business any more, or at any rate would soon not be. Once the police began taking Mona Weissman's claims seriously, as now they would have to do, Mona would no longer need any outside assistance.

An hour later, however, McIntyre had not returned.

SEVEN

"**M**OTHER, I really doubt Martin's run away from home. We got married only a month ago, he hasn't had time yet to get all that terribly unhappy with me. And even if he had, why choose that moment to go, in the middle of the night with nothing but the clothes on his back and a dead woman's dog?"

Hearing her voice begin rising, Edwina stopped talking. At the other end of the phone, her mother replied in the tones only Harriet Crusoe ever dared use upon Edwina.

"Darling, I never said a word about running away from home. All I'm saying, dear, is that Martin can perfectly well take care of himself. He's not likely to have had a fit of amnesia, is he? Young, healthy, has his checkups regularly."

Edwina was forced to agree that this much was true.

"So," Harriet concluded, "he's not wandering about in a fog, and you've checked all the hospitals. Nothing's happened to him, dear, I'm certain of it. You must simply wait for him to return.''

It was 8:00 A.M., and around Edwina the apartment seemed very bright and still, like a stage set awaiting an actor's entrance. Only the actor did not come; she had spoken with the police three times already, each time feeling an increased sense of dismay.

Maxie twined about her ankles, mewing questioningly but with no special urgency. Martin had never been Maxie's particular favorite; only for Edwina's sake, the two males tolerated one another.

But he is mine, she thought; he is my particular favorite.

"Now, darling," said Harriet, "I shall give you some advice."

Edwina shook her head impatiently; Harriet was an inveterate giver of advice. At this hour, she would be in the sun room of the big house in Litchfield, surrounded by the great clay pots of miniature tea roses transferred from the greenhouse for the summer season. Having completed what she called her pages—the writing, generally two thousand words but often more, with which Harriet occupied the hours between 5:00 and 7:00 A.M.—she would by now be answering her fan mail: the twenty or thirty gushingly enthusiastic letters she received each day from the readers of her enormously popular romance novels.

"You must occupy your mind," said Harriet

firmly. "Really, darling, you *must* keep occupied. It is the basis for everything."

Wielding her pen over sheets of engraved ecru notepaper, Harriet would be attired in a flowered silk dressing gown, high-heeled slippers, and her trademark rope of pearls too perfect and enormous to be real, her funny little secret being of course that they were real.

"Your father took off like this once," she remarked. "Have I ever told you that?"

"Mother, Martin did not take off," Edwina said, then sat up straight as the import of Harriet's words struck her. "What do you mean, Father took off? When did he take off?"

"Just before the war," said Harriet, "I absolutely thought I should go mad. Later, of course, I understood. It was secret."

Edwina blinked at the idea of her mother going mad; compared with the notion of her father "taking off," as Harriet put it, it was by far the more astonishing. Harriet's mind, or so it seemed to Edwina, resembled a shiny steel track along which her thoughts thrummed smoothly and according to strict schedule; at eight-ten, for instance—just three minutes from now—Harriet would go to the pool house for her morning swim: twenty-five disciplined laps against the ticking of a timer.

"He was gone ten days," said Harriet, "and came back a very disappointed man. The morning after he returned, Germany invaded Poland. But I'll tell you the rest another day, dear, it's time for my swim. Let me know when Martin gets there, won't you? And dear, until he does get there, do what I say: Keep occupied."

Yes, Mother, thought Edwina, knowing that Harriet was trying to be helpful. Having begun her acquaintance with McIntyre in an atmosphere of suspicion (Edwina had pots of money, Martin had none) and disdain (her pedigree traced back to Roger Williams, his to Ellis Island), Harriet had come so far in her feelings for Martin as to believe that if he vanished, it could only be on some secret mission comparable to an attempt at preventing World War II.

The brisk little click of her mother's hanging up the phone was followed by a knock on the apartment door. Edwina hurried to answer, hoping that it might mean one thing and praying that it might not mean another. But it was only Mona Weissman, whose problems Edwina had forgotten utterly for the past few hours.

"God, you look awful," Mona said. "Are you sick or something?"

"Thank you," answered Edwina, "for your concern, but I'm afraid I haven't time for conversation." She began closing the door. "I know you won't be needing me any longer, and I've already—"

"No!" Mona's reply was a gasp. "Oh, please."

Slowly, Edwina reopened the door. A girl with a faint, breathy voice, a demanding attitude, and a tenuous grasp on the most elementary rules of etiquette—the rule, for instance, requiring one to telephone ahead before showing up uninvited at a person's door—was just what she did not need this morning.

But Mona Weissman did not sound demanding now. She sounded desperate. In addition, her sloppy style of dress had reverted once more to the prim schoolgirl style she had worn at her father's memorial service—navy skirt, white blouse, sensible shoes.

"The police were at our house already," she said. "They told my mother they think my father might have been in trouble before he died. They're reopening the investigation."

"Yes," said Edwina. Pain throbbed warningly at her temples. "So, you see, you won't be needing me."

"But that's not true. The police found a dead lady—*another* dead lady."

"Yes," Edwina said again, thinking of the previous evening and wishing intensely that she might return to it. If I had not gone out there, I would not have found the dog; if I had not found the dog, Martin would not have gone out to walk it.

"They think my father might have killed her," said Mona wonderingly. "The second one, I mean. They didn't say that right out, but from the questions they were asking it was obvious they think he was involved somehow. And I can't stand it, Miss Crusoe, I just can't stand it if they . . ."

Edwina thought it was amazing what people could stand, when they were simply forced to stand it. Her own life, for example, seemed suddenly to have collapsed from beneath her like a floor constructed of tissue paper. Had McIntyre been able to return, he would have done so; therefore, he was not able to.

But from this thought her mind reeled in nauseating fright, as Mona Weissman eyed her narrowly.

"You *are* sick," Mona said. "Something's wrong, anyway. Here, you'd better sit down." Taking Edwina's arm she came in, closing the door behind her and steering Edwina to a chair.

"No, I'm fine," Edwina managed as the phone rang. She sprang up to answer and the floor took on a dreadful tilt, first one way and then the other.

"Sit," commanded Mona, "I'll get it. Put your feet up."

Edwina followed this sensible suggestion. At once the awful swimming feeling faded. Crossing the room, Mona seized the phone in businesslike fashion and spoke into it.

"Hello? Yes, Miss Crusoe is here but I'm afraid she's not able to speak with you at the moment. May I take your message?"

Edwina struggled upward; Mona waved her back. "Yes, I can tell her that. When? Yes, ten minutes will be fine. Thank you very much, officer. Good-bye."

Replacing the receiver, Mona turned to Edwina, who now lay flat out on the sofa with her feet elevated on its arm. The latest attempt to rise had sent such a swirl of giddiness through her that she thought it best to follow Mona's advice no matter what the phone call meant. Black curtains of panic kept closing in on her; straighten up, she told herself angrily, but it did no good.

"That," said Mona, "was a Detective Talbot. He says they found the dog, whatever that means, and they're bringing it over here now. I hope it's all right that I told him it was okay."

"Yes," Edwina said dully. Dear god, she thought.

"Come on, dog," said Mona Weissman, leading the panting animal to the kitchen without being asked. "Good dog, come on, we'll get you a nice drink of water."

"Hi, Edwina," said Detective Richard Talbot, removing his hat as he stepped into the apartment.

Feeling green but no longer quite so rubbery legged, Edwina led him to the living room. "Sit down, Dick. You haven't heard anything more, have you?"

Talbot had for years been McIntyre's partner until McIntyre's promotion to inspector. He was a big, broad-shouldered Irishman with blue eyes and thin black hair combed straight back from his forehead. Limping from a gunshot wound sustained five years earlier and shrunken a bit by his advancing emphysema, Talbot still possessed a voice like a straight razor, which he exercised freely on criminals, careless drivers, and anyone dumb enough to try calling him "gimpy."

"Found the dog tied to a porch rail on Orchard Street," he said. "Nothing else. I'm sorry, Edwina. I wish I could say there's progress, but look, everyone's on this, you know that."

Edwina sighed. "Thanks. Listen, has anybody thought about the case he was working on, the crazy guy who . . ."

She stopped. Of course they had.

Talbot's eyes were sympathetic. "Yeah, we thought of it. Orchard's only one street over from Beers. I won't kid you there, I don't like the coincidence much myself."

Talbot wouldn't dance you around with false optimism. A thing was what it was, good or bad; you could trust him on it.

"Tell you what, though," he went on, "I heard you spotted Fellowes last night over near Chelsea Memorial. Good place for a guy like him to hang out. Lots of different faces, plenty of places to hide, food and clothes if you know where to find 'em."

It was true; if you knew your way around or were bold and sneaky enough to learn, you could live practically forever in the buildings of Chelsea Memorial Hospital. Dietary carts stood loaded by the basement elevators, waiting for the orderlies to come and take them upstairs. Carts full of scrub suits from the laundry could be raided, and some showers still worked in the abandoned locker rooms of unused wards waiting to be renovated into office spaces.

"I guess so," said Edwina as Mona came in with a tray of tea things. Blinking in surprise, she accepted a cup of hot, sweet tea, watched while Talbot politely refused and got up, and caught the girl's enigmatic smile. Hang in there, it said, and to her surprise it made Edwina feel better.

"I guess Fellowes would think Chelsea was a good hideout."

Unfortunately there was no reason he could not leave the hospital and return to it again, if he were well disguised enough to move freely about inside. The photos on Chelsea's employee ID badges were blurry; he would need only to steal one.

"Got yourself some household help finally?" Talbot asked in tones of approval as she accompanied him to the door.

Edwina's wealth and the luxuries stemming from it had at first been the subject of razzing from McIntyre's colleagues, who to a man believed that sweeping and scrubbing were sacred wifely functions not properly delegated to employees.

Only Talbot had seen any virtue in a kind of life he could not himself afford to live, in which the doing of routine tasks by someone else simply made more time available for the doing of non-routine ones by oneself.

"No," Edwina told him, "she's a . . . friend." Out in the kitchen, Mona spoke coaxingly to Maxie and to the sheepdog. "She came over to help me while everything is . . ." But precisely what everything was went beyond her ability to describe.

"Yeah." Talbot studied his shoes. "I'll call, Edwina, anything comes up. Meanwhile you try to keep busy, get a project; you don't sit staring at the phone all day.''

All day. The words fell like two stones.

"Okay." Edwina managed to smile at him; there was no sense in making him more unhappy than he was. If anyone wanted Martin McIntyre back as much as she did, it was Talbot.

When he had gone she returned to the living room, wandered about it with the sense of having forgotten something, finally sat and drank the last of her cooling tea. Something had gone wrong, something she could do nothing to repair. McIntyre's colleagues were of course doing everything to find him; no effort of hers could possibly improve upon their professionalism.

Mona appeared in the kitchen doorway with a bottle of orange juice in her hand. From behind her came the burble of the coffeemaker, the sputter of an egg frying in a pan, and the faint sound of the radio playing. Through her misery Edwina perceived that the girl had also whisked last night's newspapers into a neat pile, started up the dishwasher, and given food and fresh water to the animals. Now Mona poured juice with one hand while popping slices of toast out of the toaster with the other.

"Listen, Mona," Edwina began, "this is all very nice of you but I don't think I'm going to be able to—"

"Eat," Mona commanded, depositing a plate of breakfast on the coffee table. "Because if you don't eat you're going to feel sick, and if you feel sick you won't be able to do anything, and then you'll just lie there stewing, won't you? And that," she concluded, "won't help anything."

Unwillingly, Edwina sipped orange juice. The bright yellow eye of the egg yolk stared sunnily at her. Reaching out, Mona cut the egg and arranged the bits of it on toast triangles where they did seem more inviting, or at least somewhat less ghastly.

"I heard the detective," she said. "I'm sorry about your husband being gone. I hope everything will be all right."

The girl did not say she was sure that Martin would turn up, for which Edwina felt obscurely grateful. The bite of egg and toast tasted good; she tried another. It was embarrassing to need to be cared for in this way, to be blindsided out of the blue by such fear that she did not know what to do; she had always been so proud of her own self-sufficiency.

Yes, said a small unpleasant voice in her head, and we know what pride goeth before, don't we?

"Anyway, the detective was right," Mona went on. "You'll be wanting something to do, to keep your mind off it. And speaking of needing something to do, I'm afraid you're stuck with me for the duration."

She smiled implacably, pouring out hot coffee from the pot. Edwina opened her mouth to object, thought better of it. Around her the enormous apartment seemed to yawn dangerously, as if it might swallow her into its silence, its unaccustomed vacancy.

That is ridiculous, she thought; I've been alone

before and in almost as terrible circumstances. But the unpleasant feeling refused to vanish, and meanwhile this odd girl intended to be helpful whether Edwina agreed or not. As if to prove this, Mona picked up the now-cleaned plate, nodding approvingly at it.

"Good," she said, "you'd be surprised how much better almost anything looks once you've got a normal blood sugar."

"What do you know about blood sugar?" Edwina asked, "and why do you care how I feel, anyway?"

Mona Weissman regarded her. "I know about blood sugar," she answered, "because I have mood swings on account of it. Well," she amended, "they're more than mood swings, they're personality changes. You must have noticed how awful I was yesterday. Like an idiot, I'd skipped dinner and breakfast. You'd think I'd know better by now.

"And," she went on, "I care how you feel because you put up with me then, even though I was behaving badly. And because you agreed to try to help me without knowing how I would pay you.

"Now," she said, still holding the plate, "you can't do anything about the trouble you're having, and I can't do anything about mine.

"But," she gestured with her free hand, "I can help you, and you can help me, and that way neither of us will be sitting around moping. So, how about a deal?"

"What kind of deal?" said Edwina. She did feel better, probably as a result of the food Mona had urged upon her. But this was no guarantee the girl's next idea would be acceptable. "What can you do that I might need besides cooking breakfasts?"

Mona grinned. As she did so, the phone rang again. At the same moment, the mail arrived, slipping in profusely through the door slot and scattering on the parquet floor.

"Feel like talking?" Mona Weissman asked, heading for the phone.

Edwina's heart thumped in mingled hope and fear. "Let the machine screen it first to see who— no, wait a minute, it could be someone who won't want to leave a message."

She did not want to think about who such a person might be. "Find out who it is. I'll talk if it's important, and then if you wouldn't mind tossing the junk mail and putting the rest of it on my desk while I take a quick shower . . ."

Striding to the phone and answering it briskly, Mona dealt with the unwanted caller in a few crisp, unyielding syllables.

"You weren't," she asked when she had hung up, "dying for a chance to find a bargain on aluminum siding, were you?"

Edwina felt disappointment flooding her. "No, I don't want aluminum siding. Or a credit card, or five-year lightbulbs, or to contribute to any of the other worthy causes that have no doubt chosen *this* morning, out of all other *possible* mornings, to harass me with their obnoxious solicitations."

Mild amusement greeted this outburst. After a moment Edwina began smiling, too. "Thank you,

Mona, for handling that for me. Perhaps we can use your help here after all. But only until my husband gets back,'' she added. "Is that absolutely understood?"

Nodding, Mona cast her glance down, in pointed parody of the humble housekeeper too cowed to meet her employer's gaze.

"Don't push it, Mona," said Edwina, noting that the girl had wit in addition to her cooking and telephone answering abilities. Perhaps she would be a good person to have around, at least until McIntyre returned.

Ruefully, Edwina realized that she simply did not want to be alone now, and that although she had friends there were none to whom she wished to admit this fact.

"When I come out," Edwina said more gently, "we'll review recent developments in your own family difficulties, shall we?"

An hour later, Mona and Edwina were in the little Fiat, headed toward Mona's house. Heat pressed down on the city like a smothering hand, turning the smallest errand into an endurance test. Still, after the things Mona had reported, Edwina felt she had little choice: Serina Weissman would have to be interviewed, and not only by the police.

"The lawyer was certain your father's will couldn't be challenged?" she asked Mona.

"Yes," Mona said positively. "Well, of course it could be challenged, but he said it would stand up. My father made it long before his illness and

before he made the contraption to kill himself.
Which," she added, "I'm still sure he never
would have used."

The girl stared unhappily ahead. "But the point
is, this is my mother's lawyer, not my father's.
And from what I overheard last night, she must
have hired him weeks ago. I guess she must have
found out about Mrs. Larsen after all."

She sighed in the superheated breeze coming in
through the Fiat's windows. Edwina would have
liked to put the top down but the sun was too
cruelly battering; already she felt flattened.

Weissman must have told his wife he was leaving her, told her too what the financial arrange-
ments would be and probably about Marcia
Larsen. Perhaps he'd even told her he was ill and
about the will he had made.

Edwina took the shore exit off the interstate,
entering an enclave of manicured greenery. At
once the heat began easing, as if amidst such
wealth its discomfort could not be tolerated and
so would not be allowed. The curving road was
lined on both sides by stone walls behind which
thick masses of shrubs hid the enormous houses,
the driveways posted with signs reading PRIVATE
and KEEP OUT. The air smelled of pines and sea
salt.

"As far as my own money goes," Mona continued, "it doesn't really look as if there's going
to be any. Everything my father left me goes into
a trust fund, and my mother is the executor of it
until I'm twenty-five. Which," she ended, "isn't
for another three years. Good as he was," her lips

twisted wryly, "I have to say my father wasn't quite up to date on our family dynamics."

Edwina glanced questioningly at her.

"My mother," Mona said matter-of-factly, "is wacko. You must have noticed that the other day. On the sauce for one thing, and not a particularly well-balanced person even when she's sober. To put it mildly," she finished.

"But you don't think there was anything wrong with your father's mental state, is that right?" Edwina took another turn, guiding the little Fiat onto a smaller and even better manicured residential street that ended at what looked like an undrivable rut but was not. NO PUBLIC BEACH ACCESS, the sign said.

Mona looked uncomfortable. "Actually I've been thinking about that, and I do think something was bothering him. A few days before he died he got kind of silent, and the look on his face was unhappy. But he had a lot to worry about, I mean I didn't know it then but now I do. And there was something else I noticed today."

The lane here was rutted and paved with rocks to discourage casual sightseers who, despite the sign, might try driving into this parklike area perched above Long Island Sound.

Mona frowned. "The police brought the car back. The one he did it in. They towed it, not down this road but around by the service drive. And the seat is in the wrong place, too far up."

Edwina glanced at the girl. "You got into the car? Mona, wasn't it—"

"Awful?" She shrugged. "No. But that was why

I did it. I had all these pictures in my head about how much blood there must be. But there wasn't, just a little spot of it.

"Only," she frowned, "the car seat wasn't where he'd have had it. It was way up practically under the steering wheel. And his hat wasn't there, I looked for it again."

"They might have moved the seat," Edwina said. "The police, you know, must have had to go over the inside of the car, so they might have moved the seat themselves."

She was surprised they had taken the car at all. Apparently McIntyre's warnings to his staff about thoroughness had sunk in. But Mona was not satisfied.

"I don't believe he killed himself, is all," she repeated stubbornly. "I just—stop here, I don't want Mother rushing out in a panic when she hears a car. You can't tell what mood she'll be in, and she's terrified of what she calls 'intruders.'"

She leaned back in the car's bucket seat and sighed. "Only I'm sure it's really that she hates for people to see her. She looks awful, or anyway she's convinced she does. I don't notice it much anymore. But the worse she looks, the vainer she gets."

Edwina pulled the car onto a patch of white pea gravel by the side of the little lane. Each corner of the patch was marked by an enormous wooden tub of red geraniums. Serina Weissman's face, she thought, was nowhere near the worst thing about her, at least to judge by Mona's clearly increasing nervousness.

"Aren't you worried," the girl asked, wringing her hands unconsciously, "that someone will call about your husband? Maybe I should just stay here and wait in case someone does try to—"

Edwina plucked up the cellular phone's handset and dropped it briskly into her carryall. "Yes, I am worried about my husband. But everyone I've talked to today has given me the same advice, and they're all right: If I don't keep moving, I'll melt into a puddle of funk. I just can't sit waiting to hear something. And my husband wouldn't want it."

That much was true. Wherever he was now, McIntyre would be hoping she was not too upset. Whatever his situation, he would be worrying about her. But from the thought of just what that situation might be, other thoughts came unpleasantly wriggling; closing her mind to these, Edwina got out of the car.

The door slam was loud in the silence. Slowly, Mona got out too and stood looking at the corner of the house, barely showing through great masses of laurel, rhododendron, and azalea.

"What about you, though?" Edwina asked as they began walking toward it. "Are you sure you want me doing this, digging around this way in your family's private life?" She looked at the girl. "Because I have to tell you," she went on, "the evidence for suicide still sounds quite persuasive to me, even with all the other things that have happened. It's physical evidence, you see, that he fired the gun. It's hard to dismiss. And . . ."

She hesitated. Clearly Weissman's death was

connected to the other two. What if he'd killed himself out of guilt, for instance? One way or another, Mona's adoring view of her father would be changed, and that seemed very sad.

". . . a number of things are beginning to trouble me," she said. "What if they're things you'd rather not have known?"

It might be worse even than Weissman really having killed himself. For instance, the physical evidence might be wrong, or misleading somehow. Mona's mother might have murdered her husband and his girlfriend—hired someone to do it, perhaps—in a rage of jealousy and for the money. That still left the woman in the garden, but . . .

There were, Edwina thought bleakly, so many possibilities, each more unpleasant than the last.

Mona's chin came up stubbornly. "Listen, I wasn't quite honest with you this morning. I don't just stick to a diet to keep my head on straight. I also take medicine, a lot of it—the kind that keeps your mind from spinning into the ozone and your feelings from falling into a pit. And I'm in regular therapy. I'm aware of the perils of reality, Miss Crusoe, and they're not as perilous as unreality, believe me. Take it from one who knows."

"I see." That, thought Edwina, was just about as sensible an answer as one could ever wish for; whatever medicine Mona was taking, it was apparently working.

The lane ended; a series of flat paving stones led down a steep slope to the back of the house, where a fieldstone terrace held cast-iron scroll-work patio furniture painted white.

"And what does your psychiatrist say," Edwina asked, "about your trying to find out more about your father's death?"

"She says two things," Mona answered. "First, that learning to live means learning to face facts, and you can't face them if you don't know them."

She kicked unhappily at some leaves on the terrace stones. "And second, if I get flaky or stop taking my pills or showing up for therapy, or if I don't eat right so I get goofy the way I did the other day and she finds out about it, she'll slap me back into the hospital so fast it'll make my head spin.

"And," Mona finished, "I believe her, which is good because if I didn't I'd have to find another psychiatrist, wouldn't I?"

She faced Edwina. "I have to know what it was all about. It can't be worse than the stories I'll make up in my head, otherwise. Knowing one bad thing isn't nearly as bad as imagining twenty, never knowing which one is really true."

You've got that one right, Edwina thought as Mona crossed the terrace and tried the back door. "Nothing you find out will make me go nuts again," the girl promised, rattling the knob. "But not finding out—well, I've got a bad feeling about that. We girls from the giggle factory just know about these things."

As she spoke a furious face had appeared at the window, its red-painted mouth twisted in a grimace at the sight of Edwina.

"Mona!" shouted the woman inside. "Who's that with you? Who did you bring here? I don't want to see any strangers!"

Mona produced a key; the lock clicked open. "Don't worry," she said, lifting her head in an attempt at bravery as the door swung wide. "She's in a tantrum, it sounds like. I guess she doesn't recognize you. But her bark's worse than her bite.

"Usually," she added, this thought proving less than wholly comforting to Edwina as, blinking in the sudden gloom of the kitchen, she followed Mona Weissman in.

At eleven in the morning Serina Weissman had not yet gotten dressed. Or perhaps she had given up getting dressed; her robe, pocked with tiny holes of cigarette burns and stained with what resembled dribbles of red wine, looked as if she might have been wearing it for days.

Her face, by contrast, was now bare of any makeup but lipstick, and looked better than it had at the memorial service. Drooping eyelids, pads of pooled silicone at the cheekbones, a dramatic sag of the right-sided facial musculature, apparently from a damaged or nicked nerve during an attempt at a radically major face-lift— Serina wasn't going to be modeling makeup for one of the big cosmetic companies any time soon, but she wasn't the horror show she thought she was, either. Without her face paints she resembled many other women her age; the facial paralysis she suffered might easily have come from a stroke, rather than from an unlucky operating-room visit.

The look in her eyes, though, was the real horror: one part resentment and one part vengefulness, laced with a touch of paranoid suspicion, like an already bitter drink tinctured with strychnine. Practically twitching in fury, Serina turned this look first upon her daughter and then upon Edwina, causing Edwina to realize in a flash why Mona needed all that therapy.

Serina picked up her glass from the littered kitchen counter and took an enormous swallow of it. Some of it leaked down her neck; she swiped at it with a clumsy hand.

"I suppose," she slurred, "you think you're so clever. You think you'll take away my things." The smell of bourbon drifted out on her words.

"Mother," said Mona soothingly, "no one's taking anything away from you. The lawyer explained it all yesterday, remember?"

Serina was quite drunk, but not too drunk to know who Edwina was once she got a good look. "You're that snooping nurse," she accused, aiming a shaky finger, "who solves the murders. I've read about you in the newspapers. You were here before, I saw you here the other day. Get out."

"Mother," Mona replied in sharper tones, "stop that. Miss Crusoe is my guest, I asked her to come here. Just because you could bully me when I was feeling bad, that doesn't mean you can get away with it all the time, you know."

Serina blinked owlishly. "I guess what I say doesn't mean much around here anymore."

Ignoring this, Mona rescued the insides of the percolator from the sink, which was heaped with dirty dishes. "Where is Mrs. Waldman, anyway?" she asked. "What's all this awful mess, and why hasn't she even helped you to get dressed yet?"

She peered narrowly at her mother. "And since when have you started drinking in the morning? Honestly, Mother, sometimes a person would think you were the crazy one around here, not me."

"I fired her," Serina replied triumphantly. "Too bossy. And I didn't start drinking in the morning: I started last night and just kept right on." She turned to Edwina. "No hangover that way," she confided.

Mona struck the heel of her hand to her forehead. "Listen, Miss Crusoe, I've got to call Mrs. Waldman and see if she'll come back. Maybe if I offer her a raise and another day off . . . Mother, why did you have to do this now?" She hurried from the room.

Seeing her go, Serina rounded unsteadily on Edwina. "You'd drink, too, if you found out your husband kept a whore," she slurred, "tried to give all his money to her, then killed himself and disgraced his entire family."

She yanked out a kitchen chair and sat down hard in it. "I don't see what I did to deserve that. I don't. I think it was very . . . very unfair."

And so much for trying to get facts out of Serina. It would be about as useful as asking questions of the whiskey bottle. Still one might as

well try. Serina sober, to judge by her perfor-
mance of the other day, was easily as bad as
Serina drunk.

"Tried to put one over on me, but he wasn't any
good at it. Everybody said Bennett was such an
honest man." She gave a harsh laugh. "Simple is
what he was. He couldn't get away with it."

Edwina pulled a chair out and sat. Around her
the big house was silent except for the murmur of
Mona's voice in another room, pleading with the
housekeeper to return.

". . . difficult, of course I do, but . . . yes, I
understand, but if I offered . . ."

Serina swayed, her pale hair falling over her
face. Unsteadily she shoved it back. "Snoop," she
pronounced clearly, "what are you doing snooping here?"

She wasn't in shape to understand any complex
reasoning. "I want to know," Edwina told her,
"why your husband didn't take the money and
leave. The half million dollars he tried to leave to
Mrs. Larsen—why didn't he just take it all himself and go?"

Serina Weissman stared, her face twitching
with what looked like fury. Tears leaked from the
corners of her eyes and slid down into the uneven
runnels of her cheeks.

Then she began laughing, a harsh wheezing
sound that fit in horridly with the shambles of her
untidy kitchen. Furnished with every sort of new
gadget and convenience, it lacked any possible
indication that anyone had ever been happy in it.
Even if it had been cleaned up, Edwina thought,

she would as soon try preparing a meal in a freshly opened tomb.

"He . . ." Serina cackled, "he . . . couldn't get it. Couldn't get his hands on a penny, I made sure of that. He'd given away a lot of money once before."

Marcia Larsen's mortgage, Edwina remembered, wondering if Serina knew where the money had gone.

"And after that I talked to a lawyer and then I said to Bennett, sign this and sign that. And like an idiot he signed."

"I'm afraid I don't understand." Mona came to the doorway, her look a mixture of pity and disgust.

"The account," Serina slurred as if this explained it all. "Not the household accounts, but the one all the real money was in. Bennett couldn't get it out unless he was dead."

She swayed. "He could *will* half," she emphasized, "but he couldn't *get* any, not in his hands. Not without my signature."

She nodded wisely, nearly losing consciousness but keeping as some drunks did her ability to form syllables. "And since the rest is tied up in this house, in our upkeep, or in my daughter's huge and quite unnecessary medical expenses . . ."

Serina blinked. "Mona had a long period of thinking that being stupid was the same as being ill, you see." One side of her lip twisted cruelly. "No one could persuade her otherwise."

"Mother," said Mona. "Mother, you are dreadful."

Serina Weissman straightened with an effort. It was like watching the last upward lurch of some sinking ship: sad, and yet one wanted it to be over.

"My husband," Serina crowed, "never got his hands on a thin dime! I made sure of that! I made . . . I made . . ."

Questioningly she peered at them, giving Edwina a clear sight of what she had been once: lovely, just for an instant.

Then two things happened: Serina Weissman passed out, and Edwina's cellular phone began buzzing from the bottom of her carryall.

EIGHT

"**T**HIS is Craig Fellowes speaking," the horrid voice said.

It had taken fewer than ten minutes to get back to town from the Weissman house after the urgent message from Talbot reporting that Fellowes had called the hospital. Now Edwina sat as Fellowes had demanded in a small conference room near the lobby in Chelsea Memorial Hospital, talking on the telephone with a murderer.

In the room with her were two plainclothes police officers, Dick Talbot, Mike Rosewater, and two nervous-looking hospital administrators. Several phones besides her own were connected by a hasty tangle of Radio Shack wires and plastic phone jacks, with Talbot listening in on one and Rosewater glowering on the other.

Go ahead, Talbot signaled, and she tried to speak, but the effort came out a croak.

"Come now, Miss Crusoe, don't be nervous with me." Fellowes sounded amused and pleased. "Just don't lie to me and everything will turn out just fine. Lying is a sin, you know, and besides I can tell. I can tell when people are lying to me."

His voice hardened on the words. From behind them came a faint metallic creaking that Edwina found familiar but could not place. "This is Edwina Crusoe," she managed.

"Good. That's good. I suppose you must wonder why I'm telephoning you, Miss Crusoe. Or am I supposed to call you," he paused meaningfully, "Mrs. McIntyre?"

She straightened, gripping the receiver with both hands. The rusty metallic creaking in the background continued.

"Is my husband all right?" Fellowes had him, must have him. Otherwise why would he have asked her such a question? She was listed as his wife and the person to call in an emergency, on the small white card in his wallet.

"He's fine," Fellowes replied. "I'm afraid he's not able to come to the phone now, though. He's all tied up at the moment." He laughed at his own stale joke, a sound made more chilling by its tone of genuine amusement.

A uniformed officer opened the door to the conference room; Talbot handed his phone to one of the plainclothes cops. Edwina could hear the murmured conversation, her mind racing along several tracks at once as the cop reported on attempts at tracing Fellowes' call.

". . . from somewhere inside, they're pretty sure. Takes time, though," the uniformed cop told Talbot. "It's a funhouse down in that switching room. Phone guys want to know can you try getting him to—"

Fellowes' voice snapped through the phone. "Who's that?"

A flood of calm washed through her; anger meant fear, and other people's fear was something she had dealt with many times. It's my own fear that gives me trouble, she realized.

"The police," she told him. "They're here in the room with me. You told them you were going to call again, you know." She kept her voice as matter-of-fact as she was able. "You must have realized they'd be here. You must have known that, didn't you?"

"Yeah." He sounded mollified. "I knew." The creaking in the background went on. Rusty, regular. Where had she heard it?

"Why are you calling me, Mr. Fellowes?"

The plainclothes officer nodded approvingly at her. Across from him Mike Rosewater gripped his own phone with an intensity suggesting his big hands might soon break it in half. He was carrying today a .38 police special in a black leather holster. All the weapons-qualified hospital security people had received their orders to carry on the job until Fellowes was brought in.

Brought in or brought down; the thought made her even more nervous than Fellowes did. Get Martin out before the shooting starts, she told herself; bullets don't have brains.

"I'm calling for the same reason everyone calls

you," Craig Fellowes said. "I want you to find me a murderer."

The plainclothes cop twirled a finger at the side of his head: nuts.

"A specific murderer." Fellowes cackled nastily. From the sound of it she knew she was losing him. The cop made a coaxing gesture; she shook her head, gesturing for a pen and paper. He's going to hang up, she scribbled as Fellowes spoke again.

"I have to go now. Can't be letting your buddies there trace me, can I? That would spoil all the fun. Although I made sure it would take them some time. Big medical center, the phone system's like spaghetti, all those wires and cables all jerry-rigged together, all those circuits and switches."

So he was in the hospital. Talbot had taken his extension back. "True," he reached past her to scribble. "Get him to call back?"

As Talbot wrote, the creaking stopped. Edwina frowned, trying to identify the clicking that came through the receiver. Next, so suddenly it took her breath away, there came a shriek of begging anguish so hideous it shot her to her feet.

"Stop that," she ordered, "stop that right this instant. Do you hear me?"

The scream stopped; the creaking sound returned. "Vengeance is mine," Fellowes whispered. "You people weren't very nice to me the last time I visited you."

The plainclothes cop stuck his head in the door again. How much longer, Talbot mouthed at him.

The cop shrugged disgustedly, held up ten fingers twice and spread his hands: who knows?

Edwina bit her lip. "My husband's not responsible for any treatment you received here, good or bad."

The pair of hospital administrators looked daggers at her; she turned coldly from their outraged stares. Chelsea Memorial had armed guards to protect its patients and its staff. McIntyre had no guards, and each minute everyone got angrier made him less safe. Even Talbot looked itchy. SWAT teams, she thought, fusillades.

It mustn't get that far; it simply mustn't. "Why did you call me, Craig? What is it you want, and what has it to do with my husband? Is it because he's the investigator on your case?"

"No. No, you've got it all wrong. Listen carefully, now, I'm only going to say this once. I know who killed the doctor, his secretary, and the other one. You find out, bring the killer to me. You do that and I'll trade with you, mine for yours."

Edwina blinked, seized the thought. Never mind how he knew, or even if he did; with a deal, he might call back. "Fine. Only not if you hurt him. If he's hurt or harmed in any way—"

"I'll decide," Craig Fellowes whispered, "who gets hurt. I apologize about what you'll find in your apartment, by the way. The devil," he finished with an audible grin, "made me do it."

Abruptly she was glad she had not left Mona Weissman there alone. But the dog was in the apartment, and Maxie.

"If you know who did all those things," she

managed around the sudden lump of worry in her throat, "why can't you just—"

"When are you people going to figure it out?" he demanded in sudden fury. "What does it take, fire and brimstone? A plague?"

"Wait," she rushed, "Craig, wait, you've got to—"

The cop stuck his head back in. "Inside for sure, we don't know where yet."

"—call back," Edwina said, "if you can't tell me where you are now."

Talbot nodded approvingly. "I mean," she hurried, feeling Fellowes' impatience, "even if I find the right person, I don't know where you are, so how can I bring you what you want if—"

"Same time, same station," Fellowes said, and hung up.

"Jesus *Christ*," said Talbot, slamming his fist onto the table, "when I get that little son of a bitch I'm going to—"

". . . nothing," said one of the hospital administrators into the telephone whose buttons he had begun punching instants after Fellowes hung up, "and I mean nothing to the press beyond the statements we've already made, not one single goddamned—"

". . . units," Mike Rosewater grated into his phone. "I don't care what the budget says, tell 'em it's mandatory double time and a half, get the staff in here and get them suited up for—"

Edwina sat staring silently down at her hands.

"Tape," said the plainclothes cop who had been on the line when the scream came through.

"I've heard a lot of this stuff," he went on kindly, "people hassling other people on the phone in all kinds of different ways. And that yell was taped, I'll make book on it. The click was a cassette machine, or maybe a—"

"Thank you," she managed, and did not point out that in order to get a scream on tape at all, someone had to scream in the first place.

Deliberately she tried not to think whether or not the voice had sounded like Martin McIntyre's. She had never heard him scream, had never in fact heard anyone make quite that horrible a sound of anguish, and she wished fervently that she had not heard it now. Listening to it had put a new gloss on her worldview, one that might take a long time to go away. If, she realized, it ever did.

She got up from the table. "I wonder if you could send an officer with me," she asked Talbot. "Just to check. He might have been bluffing when he said he'd been there, but . . ."

Talbot agreed. "You want someone to stay?" But he looked troubled; half the time there weren't enough bodies in the budget to keep a decent shift on the street.

She shook her head. "No. I'll be fine. You know me, Dick, I'll take all the precautions. Having your guys there will just make me more anxious about . . . everything."

And limit my activities, too, she thought. Talbot eyed her with skepticism, but gave in. "And look, all that stuff about trading," he added, "that's a story we're giving him, all right? That's all. You got him to say he'd call back, that's good work right there, so take a vacation on the rest of it."

He patted her awkwardly on the shoulder. "I know how that sounds," he added in tones of apology, "but it's orders from above. You're to stay out of it. If it were up to me . . ." He lifted his hands and let them fall.

"Sure, Dick," she said, not looking at him.

On the way back to the apartment, she asked the officer driving her to stop at the locksmith's in the shopping plaza next to her high-rise. The shop smelled sweetly of burnt metal from the key machine, three-in-one oil from the repair bench. Mitchell Brandt greeted her heartily, looking up from the set of keys he was making for a pretty blonde woman in a red sundress.

All around on pegboard displays hung shiny hardware, from doorchains and simple locksets with cylinders to the case-hardened intergrip rim locks Mitch sold to people who wanted real security rather than just the appearance of it.

"I'll wait," she told him, and he nodded before turning back to his work. It was Mitch who had assembled her handy kit of lock-picking instruments.

Gone, she thought angrily, by another official decree. Out of it, indeed.

"Don't be leaving these under the doormat, now, or in the mailbox," Mitch warned the woman. "I don't know why I'm making you all these keys, you lose 'em, pretty soon burglars have 'em, then anybody can get into your place who finds out where it is.''

The woman agreed, took her keys and paid for them. Mitch Brandt shook his head, watching her go out.

"But hey, how's anybody gonna know where she lives, she's thinkin', right? She don't know her boyfriend, he's the biggest bum in town."

He put his hands flat on the counter. "I mean," he added, "she don't know yet. And I sure am not the guy who's gonna tell her, get that big lug mad at me. I know him from the old days. She gives him a key, he's copyin' that sucker, and by the end of the week he's sellin' his old lady's stuff."

Mitch looked sad. "Crime ain't what it used to be, Edwina. There was honor among thieves. Hey, what can I do for you?"

Mitch was a fireplug-shaped man with a mug of a face and quick, flighty fingers that looked as if they belonged on someone else: a surgeon, maybe. Once he had worked the other side of the fence, unlocking tricky locks for people who did not own the things those locks protected. But that was long ago. These days, he thwarted the guys whose able assistant he once had been, and his face darkened now as Edwina told him her story.

"Sure," he said when she had finished, "just let me go get Mandy. I'll come right on up to your place with you."

Edwina waited by the counter while Mitch disappeared through a door at the back of the workroom. Outside, the uniformed cop waited patiently in the squad, not averse to a little easy duty. From the back of the shop came a sharp yelp of greeting and then Mitch appeared again. At his heel trotted an enormous German shepherd whose massive head swiveled suspiciously as it caught Edwina's scent.

"Umph," it grunted quietly, stopping short, no friendliness at all in its deep-throated tone or in its watchful, waiting eyes. Its head would have looked the right size perched upon the shoulders of a fair-sized moose, only no moose Edwina had ever seen could curl its upper lip back quite so threateningly to expose so very many sharp white teeth.

When Mitch said nothing, busy closing up his cash drawer, the dog took a stiff-legged step toward the front of the shop, its gaze fixed firmly on her throat. "Umph," it said again, and this time there was positively no mistaking its meaning, or its immediate, extremely violent intent.

"Mandy," said Mitch indulgently, glancing at the animal. "You be a good girl, now, Edwina is our friend. Go say hello to her." He dropped some metal items into his toolbox, thought a moment, and added a few more.

"Mandy," Edwina said faintly as the dog advanced upon her. "Uh, Mitch, are you sure she's going to be . . ."

Mandy whined, tipping her head in winsome greeting, pink tongue lolling from her enormous mouth. Then she sat down hard, gazing up in adoration as her weight threatened to fracture a number of small but important bones in Edwina's right foot.

"Oof." Edwina laughed in spite of herself, mostly out of relief, and with an effort freed her foot from the dog's massive bulk. "Come on, dog, you're heavy." In reply, Mandy shoved her big head beneath Edwina's hand, wriggling with friendliness.

Mitch snapped his kit shut. "Okay, let's go stop the bad guys." He spied the squad out his front window, rolled his eyes and shrugged. "Been a long time since I got a free ride in one of those things." He began shutting the shop's lights off; the dog headed expectantly ahead of him for the front door.

"Mitch, I hate to say this but I don't think Mandy can come along," Edwina said. "There's a cat and dog in my place already."

Mitch Brandt laughed. "She's not coming." He slipped the dog a biscuit. "Watch 'em, girl," he told her, "watch 'em, now."

The animal snapped to attention, still chewing the biscuit. A low whine escaped her powerful jaws as she reduced the treat to powder. Her face aligned itself in an expression of ferocity as Edwina took a quick step back, finding the dog's look as utterly convincing as it was professionally bloodthirsty.

"Locks, they're for people outside," said Mitch. "Mandy is for any of 'em who happen to get inside. It's my own little security system," he confided, "and it works like a charm."

Unfortunately, Edwina's own dog—or at least the one she now possessed, no friend or relative having stepped up to claim Marcia Larsen's pet—had no such idea of functioning as part of a security system. Two steps into her apartment, Edwina had this fact impressed forcefully and unhappily upon her by the number of papers, dishes, books, lamps, pieces of furniture, and items of clothing strewn everywhere about the place.

No search had taken place; this was malice, pure and simple. And Maxie was nowhere to be found. The squad car cop, his hand poised at his weapon, phoned to ask crime-scene people to go over the place in case it contained some physical evidence of Fellowes' trespass on the apartment.

"Crikes," said Mitch Brandt, "they've got murders on this loony tune, now they're gonna spend all that time workin' up a little break an' enter?"

He waited in the shambles of the kitchen, not touching anything lest his own fingerprints should later be recovered from some innocent object; not that he was likely to be a suspect, but with a past like his one never could be too cautious, and he did know how to get into places—a fact of which the New Haven cops were still aware to judge by the look he got from the scene team people when they all trooped in.

"Do the door first, please, I want Mr. Brandt to work on it," Edwina asked the woman officer in charge of lifting prints.

As the woman got down to business with her spray cans, magnetic brush, and tin of magnetic powder, the other officers moved about peering at things and photographing them, finding little of interest.

Also, they did not find Maxie. The dog, however, soon made his presence felt by howling from inside the hall bathroom.

"Go ahead," said the fingerprint woman in disgust, "we're not going to get anything. The creep wiped everything he touched."

"How can you tell?" Edwina paused on her reluctant way to get the dog out, curious about what the technician was doing now.

"See here, with this magnetic brush you don't use ordinary fingerprint powder. It's fine iron filings; you just put some on the brush. So you don't leave a lot of mess, and you can cut a wide swathe on a surface and kind of keep your eyes open."

She indicated the white-enameled inside of the doorframe. "See how all these prints show up? All kinds, from people going in and out. But here, no one wipes like this for cleaning. This is where someone didn't want his prints lifted, and I'll bet it's the same wherever our joker touched."

She sighed and dug in a canvas satchel for a camera. Edwina recognized the Polaroid CU-5, a fixed-focus 1 × 1 that had become standard gear for the fingerprint technician since Vernon Geberth had recommended it in his homicide investigation textbook.

"I'll take some snaps," the fingerprint tech said, "but I don't expect much. Real sweetheart we're dealing with."

I, thought Edwina clearly, I'm dealing with him. He didn't go to your house or take your husband. He didn't call you up to taunt you on the telephone. It's me he's done those things to.

A call from the back bedroom distracted her; ignoring the dog's cries—if Maxie were alive in there his howls would be louder than the dog's, and if he were dead she did not think she could bear it—she hurried to see what new outrage had been discovered.

The room was a spare room, full of things for which places could not be found elsewhere: a daybed too uncomfortable for the guest room but perfect for the unwelcome visitor who might be relegated to this chamber, the word processor McIntyre had bought but found that he despised, paperback books for browsing in the event of boredom, and a clutter of rugs, lamps, and pictures from the Litchfield house, all too good to throw out but too odd to be assimilated comfortably in any household possessing fewer than twenty rooms.

Nothing had been disturbed, but because of the room's normal disarray the evidence technician had not been able to be sure of this. Now he lay on his stomach peering frustratedly into the space beneath the daybed.

"Here, kitty," he said.

"Oh," said Edwina softly, dropping flat herself.

Maxie blinked from the darkness at her, crouched beneath the bedsprings just out of her reach. He seemed neither harmed nor frightened, only reluctant to abandon whatever it was that he had clutched between his two front paws.

"Murp," he pronounced contentedly, mouthing what seemed to be but of course could not possibly be a small stuffed animal.

"Can't quite see what he's got there, but he's okay," said the evidence technician, who seemed satisfied with his find, and Edwina felt a rush of warmth for him.

"Oh, thank you, I was—" She stopped as Maxie shifted his grip and the nature of his plaything became clear to her.

"—worried about him," she finished smoothly, and got up from the floor. The evidence technician stood, too, smiling in spite of the floor lint clinging to his suit.

"Nothing much interesting in here," he said, "only got down to take a look when I heard him purring. I've got cats at home myself, three of 'em. Want me to fish him out for you?"

"Um, no, thank you. Why don't we just leave him under there for now, so he won't be in people's way while they're working?"

"Good idea," the evidence technician said, and it was not until after he and the others had gone and Mitch Brandt was busy changing door locks that Edwina went back to the spare room, and lay down on the floor to peer under the bed again.

"Maxie," she said, and the cat looked up happily at her, as if to say that while he did not much like strange people, the strange gifts they left sometimes turned out to be very enjoyable indeed. The soft white object entertaining him now, for instance, was quite unlike any catnip-stuffed novelty item Edwina or McIntyre had ever brought him.

This Edwina thought quite understandable, for the thing he had between his paws was not stuffed with catnip. Rather, it was stuffed with rat entrails, the reason for this being that it was a real rat. Not, however, an ordinary rat; this was an extremely hairy white lab rat. Also, it was an extremely dead white lab rat.

Craig Fellowes, it seemed, had not been bluffing when he said he knew something about the deaths of Bennett Weissman, his secretary, and the woman found in Marcia Larsen's garden. Nor had he entered her apartment merely for the enjoyment of wreaking havoc in it, to frighten her and show her what he could do if he chose.

She could not imagine why Fellowes cared about the killings, what he wanted or was trying to prove. But he had come here to do more than inflict random torment.

He had come here, Edwina felt sure, to leave her a clue.

Half an hour later, Edwina regarded the spotless vacancy of Vinnie Perillo's lab, empty now of everything he had owned. No scampering rats in cages, no heaps of glassware washed or unwashed, no notes of his experiments scattered like trash about the room. It was as if Perillo had never been here.

Which was probably just the way he wanted it to be, since it was obvious what had happened: Vinnie had made a run for it. But why? She hadn't said anything to him to get his wind up. Surely sitting tight would have been his best bet whatever he was or was not guilty of.

One of the clinic buildings' housekeepers came

out of the lab, carrying a dustpan and pushing a trash bin on wheels. Dressed in a shapeless gray dress and smock, the housekeeper was old, wiry, and intent on her next task.

"Nobody here," the housekeeper said, brushing back a few strands of gray hair. "I wouldn't be here myself, but the office, they say there'll be a new man comin' in, place got to be all spic an' span right quick. Space is tight around here."

"That was fast," Edwina said distractedly. So Vinnie hadn't just headed for the hills without a word to anyone; he'd resigned, or at least officially given up his research place. What could have made him do so?

The housekeeper just stood there, a look of mild patience on her face, until Edwina stepped back out of the way. As she did, she glimpsed what was in the dustbin.

"Excuse me. I'm terribly sorry, but . . . may I have that?" She plucked out a copy of Bennett Weissman's new journal issue, still in its paper mailing wrapper. Other copies, unwrapped, lay crumpled among the trash, all of which she longed to root through. But she would have to be satisfied with this; the housekeeper's look was growing less patient by the moment.

The dustbin's wheels rumbled gently away down the corridor. "Wait," Edwina called, and the housekeeper turned, long suffering.

"I wonder," Edwina asked her, "do they issue you keys? I mean, you must have to get into a lot of places. After hours, I mean. I know you work terrible hours."

The housekeeper stood there without replying, apparently waiting for Edwina to reveal what was on her mind. She had, her face said, no time for silly guessing games.

"What I want to know is about the office down the hall, the one with the new lock. I want to know when it was put there. On Dr. Weissman's office, that is. The journal office where the doctor's secretary was—"

"Killed," said the housekeeper. "I know the one you mean." She regarded Edwina flatly. "Don't know when the lock was put on there. Got a new key two weeks ago. Guess I won't be using it much anymore, though. That office's going to be torn out, put a bunch of them new computers in there, not much cleanin' going to be needed. That," she finished, "is what they call progress."

She turned and resumed her slow departure down the hall. After a moment Edwina took the journal issue into Vinnie Perillo's abandoned lab, sat down on a low counter by the room's single window, and began to read. She had finished Vinnie's article and begun on the first of several commentaries Bennett Weissman had run along with it when a young woman appeared in the doorway, looking furious.

"If you're a friend of his, he's not coming back," the young woman said.

She didn't sound sorry about it. Tall and slender, with very white skin and the kind of red hair that escapes its pins no matter what attempts are made to tame it, the woman had pale blue eyes and hands clenched in angry fists. Her mouth, which looked as if it were accustomed to smiling, was set now in a tight thin line.

As she stalked in, her glance fell on the journal issue. "You, too? The whole building's reading it, everything's at a dead stop. You'd think it was the *National Enquirer*, which is where I suppose we'll all be written up next week."

She glared around. "He took my coffeemaker, too, that little bastard. I swear, if I ever get my hands on him, I'll kill him."

Edwina got up. The girl—at closer inspection she could not have been more than nineteen—wore a T-shirt and blue jeans topped by a stained and ragged lab coat. On her feet were a pair of white high-top sneakers.

"It does," said Edwina, gesturing with the journal issue, "look quite awful. Is anyone else going to get hurt by this?"

The piece Vinnie had published in Bennett Weissman's journal was filled with a great many long, complex sentences, the logical transitions between these consisting more of intuitive leaps than of actual scientific reasoning, at least to Edwina's eye. Also, it was almost entirely devoid of evidence: no tables, no numbers, no statistics, nothing.

The girl shrugged, hands on her hips as she stared around. "Oh, hey, no. Just anyone who ever was associated with him in any way, that's all. Only our whole department. I mean look at the thing, it makes us all look like idiots. This was my summer research project, but I wish I'd gone to work at Burger King."

It was in fact quite embarrassing. Edwina had not been able to think why Bennett would have published it, until she paged on to the accompanying review commentaries. These three critiques by experts in the fields of dermatology, endocrinology, and genetics ripped Vinnie's so-called work up one side and down the other with a ferocity Edwina had rarely seen equalled.

And that, of course, was the point: the only reason for any of it to have appeared was to make a fool of Vinnie, publicly and emphatically.

"You mean here?" she asked. "You worked with Vinnie?"

The girl shook her head. "No, thank god, that was Caroline. She was lucky, though, she got out. Just quit flat on him last week, never came back in."

"Oh," said Edwina softly, thinking that perhaps Caroline hadn't been so lucky after all.

The girl pried a thumbtack from a bulletin board and removed the last removable thing in the lab, a Sierra Club calendar whose August photograph showed a grove of birch trees with a river running through it.

"This is mine," she said. "And I'm supposed to lock this room until the new guy gets here, please god he's not another jerk. Although I guess the one I'm really mad at is Weissman."

Edwina went out obediently and stood as the girl locked up with a key from an enormous metal ring of them.

"I mean," the girl went on, "just because Vinnie nagged at him and nagged at him to publish his so-called research, that's no reason to make a public fool out of the guy, and all of us along with him. Why couldn't Weissman have just told Vinnie what an idiot he'd be making of himself?''

"Perhaps," said a voice from behind them, "Dr. Weissman knew Vincent would not believe him.''

The silver-haired man was slim and dapper in a pinstriped suit; a white linen handkerchief peeped from his pocket, and his air of calm competence was marred only by a look of worry.

"The whole affair," he told Edwina ten minutes later, "was meant to teach a lesson to Vincent, but I fear the attempt has backfired.''

His name was Smith and he was a gentleman's gentleman, what one used to call a valet. But this fit, fiftyish man was much more than a servant, she felt sure, as sitting in the passenger seat of his large dark car she watched the neighborhood change from steamy downtown bustle to tree-lined residential streets.

"So Vincent's father knew Weissman would do this to him?" Smith reminded her of the men her own father had brought home on occasion: quiet and polite, their faces betraying little as they vanished with their briefcases into the library or the study. Hours later they would emerge as unrumpled as if they had been sitting motionless all that time, with only a whiff of something like electricity lingering in the rooms through which they had passed.

"No one did anything to Vincent that Vincent

did not arrange to have done to himself," replied Smith with a touch of asperity. "But yes, his father knew. Mr. Perillo and Dr. Weissman were old friends, and when Vincent approached Weissman with his claims, the doctor called Mr. Perillo, wondering how to handle it."

"Their solution being to make him a laughingstock. Doesn't that strike you as a little harsh?"

Smith shook his head. "I was not consulted." He turned into an unmarked drive leading up to two granite pillars, braked before an iron gate, and faced Edwina.

"Mr. Perillo didn't hire me twenty years ago to rely on my advice, but to carry out his orders regarding his son. It was about the time the Getty boy was taken; perhaps you're too young to remember, but the episode struck panic into wealthy parents. My job was thwarting kidnappers, warning off bad companions, that sort of thing."

"So thanks to you, he survived adolescence without having his ear cut off and mailed to his father in a box. But what was supposed to happen once the journal came out and his career was destroyed?"

Smith pushed a button on the dashboard; the iron gates swung open and the car moved between them. "He was to go home. His father has a job waiting for him. Advance copies of the journal are not distributed. In the past they have had a tendency to destabilize the prices of pharmaceutical stocks, so Dr. Weissman kept close tabs on them. But Mr. Perillo had managed to get this one."

"And to read the commentaries to Vinnie," she guessed. Ahead, the house appeared, an enormous old Victorian with gingerbread trim, freshly painted in cream and vermillion, nasturtiums and white petunias tumbling from its windowboxes.

"Correct," said Smith, pulling the car to a halt. "On the telephone last night, to make Vincent see reason and take the job his father offered. Not," he added, "a science job. One on the administrative side of the business, I gather."

He got out of the car, as did Edwina. "But Vinnie didn't take it. He didn't run home with his tail between his legs, as his father had expected."

"No, he didn't." Smith looked troubled. "He waited until I'd gone for the evening. Then, apparently, he gathered a few of his things, went to clear out his lab and write his resignation, and . . ."

He paused, gazing up at the house, which to Edwina had begun resembling a gilded cage. Then what he'd said struck her.

"You'd gone? And why read the piece to Vinnie on the phone? Doesn't he live here with his—"

"What?" Smith came back to himself. "Oh, heavens no. His father doesn't live here, nor do I. This is Vincent's house, he lives here alone. Or," he amended unhappily, "he did live here. Please, Miss Crusoe."

He stepped aside to let her go ahead up the porch steps, onto the shady front porch furnished in white wicker. From inside came chamber music and the smell of cookies baking.

"The housekeeper," Smith explained, opening the screen door. "Do please come in," he added. "I've been all through the place, but my eye is so accustomed to everything here. Perhaps you'll be able to see some detail I've missed. Something," he finished, "that might tell me where Vincent has gone."

Inside, the house was as beautifully kept as out, with shining hardwood floors, trim painted in historically correct colors, the heavy old Victorian furnishings upholstered in dark velvets and swagged in gold. Not until the upstairs came into view was there any evidence that Vinnie lived here at all, but here he was present with a vengeance in the stark white walls and fluorescent lighting, in the reek of bunsen burners and the litter of notebooks, in the sense of an obsession patiently pursued.

In Vinnie's workroom a microscope stood on a lab bench, the rest of the room fitted out in the same high-tech style. On the walls hung his diplomas, all from the kinds of institutions where things could not be faked, or not for long. Vinnie had earned the honors represented here. His bedroom was a mattress, a bureau, and a reading lamp; a third room held nothing but books.

She flipped through a few of them; the science in them was far beyond her. In his bedroom she glanced at notebooks filled with notes, again finding them too advanced for her understanding. There was nothing here to help her locate him, nothing in fact to suggest that it was worth hunting for him. To judge by his place, Vinnie Perillo was a man with a single interest and it did not include administering the business side of a pharmaceutical company.

Also, it did not include murder. No diary, no items from Weissman's office, nothing linking Vinnie with Marcia Larsen; likewise nothing to connect him with an ex–lab technician named Caroline. The target shooting Vinnie had mentioned was apparently accomplished with a BB pistol, and not recently; the gun lay on a shelf gathering dust. There was nothing in any of the rooms to suggest where Vinnie might be now.

Smith accompanied her silently through her tour; when she had finished and they stood outside again, she confronted him.

"Mr. Smith, I have not been completely frank with you. I have my own reasons for wanting to find Vinnie. And when I tell them to you, you may not be very happy with me. You know about the murder of Dr. Weissman's secretary, I suppose?"

Smith nodded. "Of course. I read of it in the newspapers this morning. That is also how I know of you and of your excellent reputation."

"What about Vinnie's lab assistant? Has he mentioned that she'd quit?"

"Yes," Smith said cautiously, "he told me she'd walked out in a huff. But I don't quite see . . . oh. Oh, dear, yes I do see. Oh, my."

"That's right. I believe the police will soon be looking for Vinnie. When they find him, they'll question him about two and possibly three murders. I need to find him before they do, and you, I gather, would like to find him before his father does."

"Perhaps," Smith said slowly, "we might help one another?"

"Maybe. But you'd better hear the rest of it first." Quickly she told him of Craig Fellowes and Martin McIntyre, about Fellowes' apparent belief that Vinnie *had* done murder, and about Fellowes' demand for a trade.

"So if you do locate Vincent, you mean to keep your end of your deal with this person," Smith said.

"Right. Unlike the police; to them it's just a way to buy time, find out where Fellowes is hiding and fake him out somehow. My plan, by contrast, is to deal with him—long enough, anyway, to get my husband safe."

Smith nodded again. The grounds of Vinnie's little estate were cool and peaceful, a few birds twittering here and there in the deep shrubbery, protected from the afternoon heat. The idea of handing Vinnie over to a sociopath didn't seem to be giving him much pause, which made Edwina wonder just how bad the elder Perillo's wrath could be. Bad enough, Smith seemed to think, to make saving Vinnie from it a thing worth doing, even at the cost of his own job and considerable danger to Vinnie himself.

"Why," Smith asked, "do you not simply trust the police?"

She shook her head impatiently. "I trust them. It's just that I know how these things go. People get excited, they start shooting, and people get hurt. I don't want that to happen."

People, she thought, like Martin McIntyre. The idea turned her urgently toward the car.

"I don't know if Vinnie's committed murder," she repeated, "but Fellowes thinks he has, and the police are going to. Especially when his lab tech turns up dead, which I'm rather sure she will. A body's been found," she explained to his look of dismay. "It's just a matter of identification."

"Worse," Smith murmured, "and worse."

"Once this is all over," she said, "I'm willing to try to help Vinnie. I can't save him from prosecution. But we may find a way to allow the authorities to go easier on him, if, for instance, he helps to rescue a police officer. I might even intercede for him with his father."

At Smith's expression of skepticism, she had to laugh. "Don't worry, I've bearded worse lions in their dens. Only, Vinnie has to help me first. And before *that*, we have to find him."

Smith studied his highly polished black shoes. When he looked up, there was resignation in his eyes. "Jail, or an accountant's career. I suspect even a madman would look good to Vincent, next to that. All right, Miss Crusoe, if we find him I'll try to persuade him. That's all I can promise you."

A push of the dashboard button swung the iron gate inward, and when they had passed it closed again. Edwina leaned against the soft leather of the big car's front seat. "You know, there's just one thing I still don't understand. Vinnie is not a stupid person. He is in fact a well-trained and talented researcher, even a gifted one. Yet if what you've told me and what I've seen is true, he's deluded himself into believing he's made major scientific discoveries, ones other workers say must be nonsense."

Smith glanced at her. "Miss Crusoe, are you familiar with a type of literature known as science fiction? In it, a single theme is frequently presented, that of a primitive civilization regarding a science far beyond its own ken as magic."

"Oh," said Edwina. "You mean . . . ?"

"Vincent has explained it to me," he said, "and although of course I did not understand many of the details, I must say that if I had to bet my life on his work, I would do so without qualm. He is sheltered, unworldly, and socially inept. But he is brilliant. And he insists that he is right. I, for one, believe him."

Edwina sat absorbing this. After a moment Smith spoke again. "You said that you planned to find Vincent and hand him over to this other man, this killer. If I may be so bold as to ask, in what way have your plans been altered, now?"

Outside, soft suburban greenery changed back to the gritty gray of city streets, the last of the afternoon's sun hammering down upon them. "I still mean to find him," she answered. "And I'll still trade him away for my husband's safety, if I can."

Smith was a most responsible caretaker, and he clearly loved Vinnie, whom she thought fortunate indeed to have such a loyal friend. It was this loyalty, in fact, that decided her: What was one more drop of trouble in an ocean of it?

"Only now," she promised, "I'll get him back for you."

NINE

IF any missing-persons reports had been filed on the absent lab tech named Caroline—if she did not live alone, if she had a boyfriend, if her mail were piling somewhere in a noticeable heap—then it would not take long for the remains found buried in Marcia Larsen's garden to be identified.

And that, thought Edwina, could mess up her entire plan, as it would surely make the police want to interview Vinnie, and put them on the hunt for him once they realized he'd disappeared. How Craig Fellowes knew what Vinnie had done and, for that matter, why and even whether Vinnie had done it—Weissman's death was one thing, but Marcia Larsen and the lab technician didn't quite add up—were questions for another day. What she needed now was Vinnie himself, before anyone else started looking for him very hard.

"Edwina," said Harry Lemon, his face troubled, "are you sure you shouldn't just let the police take care of all of it? Not," he added hastily, "that I doubt your competence or the excellence of your plan, but it is so . . ."

"Rash, foolhardy, dangerous, and utterly apt to fail," said Edwina miserably. "Pick your adjective, Harry, I'm a thesaurus of pessimism at the moment."

They sat at a corner table in the cafeteria of Chelsea Memorial Hospital, where Smith had dropped her off with a promise to telephone her if he should find Vinnie or if anything helpful should occur to him. Activity throughout the day had kept Edwina reasonably hopeful and buoyant, but now outside the big room's tall plate glass windows evening was falling. She twirled a spoon in a cup of coffee and wondered if Harry might be right.

Across from her, Harry dug hungrily into his chicken potpie and chewed with businesslike efficiency. At this hour, nurses and technicians streamed between the cash registers, carrying trays and hurrying to tables to make the most of their half-hour break. Among them visitors moved hesitantly, peering at little dishes of cottage cheese and fruit, lingering over the choices at the steam tables as if one might be better than another, which was not the case.

"Harry, if I tell the police about Vinnie, they'll find him faster than I can, and arrest him."

Harry nodded. "And so they should." He buttered a dinner roll and bit into it. "You ought to eat," he pointed out.

"So I've been told, thank you, but I already have someone trying to stuff food into me. Which reminds me, I told Mona I'd pick her up, she's still out there with that god-awful mother of hers. But Harry, you weren't there listening to Fellowes. I was and I think he means it, I think he'll trade Martin for Vinnie."

"I think by tomorrow he'll decide he's Napoleon or Leonardo da Vinci, and not remember a word he said to you today. Besides, if you don't tell the police and Vinnie gets out of the country, or worse, gets killed by that maniac, you are going to be in deep and serious difficulty, Edwina. And what if Martin gets hurt?"

She nodded unhappily. "I don't know how I'd even get Vinnie to go along with it. I've been thinking of hitting him over the head and dumping him in a laundry hamper, wheeling him wherever Fellowes says I ought to bring him." She bit her lip very hard.

Harry looked up. "Now, now, I shouldn't have said that about Martin. I know you won't do anything to put him in danger, and perhaps Fellowes will remember. Here, have a bite of my cake. It's good, this frosting is pure processed sugar."

He held it out on a clean fork, so entreatingly that Edwina opened her mouth, and he popped it in. "See? Gives you energy. Yum, yum."

She managed a smile. "Fellowes said he wouldn't call till tomorrow, so I guess I shouldn't be—"

Just then as if by some malignant kind of thought transfer, the cellular telephone in her bag thweeped twice. Stiffening her spine with an effort, she dug it out, pressed the answer button, and listened as Fellowes' voice came through tinnily.

"Just to let you know I'm thinking about you. I'm keeping my end of our bargain. Your husband is fine, just fine."

Edwina spoke dry-mouthed. "Let me talk with him, please. I really need to know—"

"You don't need to do anything, Miss Crusoe, except exactly what I tell you. I'm going to phone you tomorrow as we arranged, only not at the time we arranged. One hour earlier, and straight to you on your little phone gadget. Your husband gave me the number. All right?"

"Yes. All right." Harry was watching her carefully.

"When I do call, I'll tell you when and where to deliver our culprit. You do know who I mean? You got my message earlier?"

The rat, he meant. "Yes, I know. But what if I can't find the person you want by the time you—"

Fellowes laughed. "I think you'd better. I really do think so. But don't worry too much about it, Miss Crusoe. I have an interest in all this as well, you know. And I sense our friend is closer than you think. As," he finished, "am I."

He hung up. Edwina stared across the table at Harry. "You won't tell anyone," she said. "Promise me, Harry. I need to be able to run things by you. You're logical and smart and I need someone to bounce things off, but I also need to know I can trust you."

Reluctantly, Harry nodded. People at nearby tables were glancing at her curiously. Feeling spotlit, she got up, heading for the exit. "My logical smartness," Harry said, hurrying after her, "tells me that if I'm not careful, I'm an accessory before the fact of whatever is going to happen. Just remember I'm in legal troubles enough already, all right? Do endeavor not to land me in a jail cell if you can help it."

"Heavens, I forgot." She turned. "Harry, I'm so sorry, I didn't even ask about your problems. I'll call my lawyer friend at once." She dug in her bag for Hansford Meredith's card. "He must be at home by now."

"Don't bother. I called him already. Set up an appointment for tomorrow, assuming my customers don't all conveniently choose tomorrow to worsen their horrendous medical conditions."

They stood before the main bank of elevators with the usual early-evening lobby crowd swirling around them: surgeons trying to make it to dinner before the cafeteria's grill shut down, staff and visitors headed back to the wards to resume getting in one another's way up there, uniformed guards looking unusually grim and alert, scanning anyone who came into the hospital through the big double glass front doors.

"Dr. Lemon," snapped an elderly black woman wearing a flowered silk dress and a black straw hat. She stepped up very near to Harry and poked her finger at his chest. "Listen here, I want to talk to you."

Harry sagged. "Mrs. Remington." His eyes

gazed in appeal over the woman's head; recognizing the name, Edwina realized this was the mother, or perhaps the aunt or grandmother, of the patient whose family was suing Harry. Whatever she was, she was very angry, backing Harry into the elevator and talking at him a mile a minute.

Please, Harry's eyes said. Reluctantly Edwina got into the elevator, too, and pushed the button for the seventh floor.

". . . nothing right, I mean not a single thing right, and I think you should do something about it. You can't just give up on a boy like that, leave him to shift for himself. You're his doctor. What did you let a thing like that happen for? Didn't you take some kind of an oath not to let things like that happen? I don't mean the bleach, you know I don't blame you for that. I'm the *only* one who doesn't. I mean what's happening *now*."

Slowly the elevator rose. "Mrs. Remington, I'm not your son's doctor anymore," Harry said. "I'm off the case, do you understand? The hospital's not going to keep me involved with his care at a time when his family is suing me, saying that I already took care of him badly. It just wouldn't be . . ." His plump pink hands sawed the air helplessly. "Prudent," he finished.

Mrs. Remington planted her hands on her hips. "Prudent? Where do you get the nerve to talk to me about prudent, my boy is losing his life? *I* am not suing you, that's those cousins of his, *they're* the ones had the idea to be suing you. And there's not a one of them got the brains God gave a pan of warm milk, which I don't see how that lawyer they hired doesn't see that, either, smart as he's supposed to be."

The elevator doors opened onto the seventh floor. "And I don't care who tells you that you are not my son's doctor. We both know who his doctor is, who has been his doctor ever since he first got sick. And you," she finished, poking Harry again, "are it."

Herding Harry down the corridor, Mrs. Remington made little gestures like a woman shooing a chicken into a coop. Bemused, Edwina followed.

"So don't you be telling me that you are not his doctor, now," she warned as Harry tried unsuccessfully to get a word in. "You know it, I know it, and the Lord knows it, so you scoot!"

Harry stopped before one of the patient rooms, drawing himself up stubbornly. "Mrs. Remington, am I to understand you are not satisfied with the care your son is receiving? Because the team in charge of his case is very competent, I don't see—"

"You look," snapped Mrs. Remington, pointing. "You just look in there, and you tell me."

Sighing, Harry obeyed. Silently, Edwina peered past him also. The private room was dim, one small lamp burning on the bedside table. In the bed lay a man so thin his shape barely disturbed the neat, taut blanket. Tubing that protruded from his mouth was connected to a respirator; with each gentle whushing sound from the machine, his chest rose and fell.

On the bedside table was a Bible; on the wall opposite hung a large paint-by-numbers oil portrait of Jesus. A tape player on the windowsill was playing the Mormon Tabernacle Choir's rendition of the Twenty-third Psalm.

"Good heavens," Harry breathed, "are those cousins trying to kill him outright?"

"That," replied Mrs. Remington, "was what I said. But of course I am just an old lady, they think I don't know anything. I get off work, I come straight over, and this is the way I find him, laid out like for a funeral."

Harry snapped off the tape machine. The man in the bed sighed deeply, as if with relief. "Mrs. Remington, can you get the cousins to call off that infernal lawsuit against me?"

He snatched the Bible from the table, yanked the portrait from the wall, and snapped on the television that hung from the ceiling on a bracket, tuning it to the all-sports station with the volume up. "It's just until I can get you some decent music, Willie. Hang in there with the Mets for a while, okay? They're two games out of first place."

The man in the bed did not stir. On the television, Howard Johnson hit a fly ball to left, and the crowd went wild.

"I can't get them to do nothing," Mrs. Remington said in disgust. "They got themselves a sniff of money, and you know that money is purely worse than heroin. And that lawyer fellow is encouraging them, too. He says you sure have done wrong."

She shook her head. "I want to see *him* come in here and shake some life back into Willie like *you* have all those times, and for all their churchgoing ways those cousins of his . . ."

She made a rude sound. "You want me to go home, get some of Willie's tapes? That Miles Davis, Willie sure likes him."

Harry's eyes gave the room a final professional once-over; then, with his hands full of religious objects, he came back into the corridor. "You do that," he said. "And get some posters of women if you can find them. You know the kind I mean, something scandalous, just in case he happens to open his eyes."

She didn't flinch. "I know. I'll get them. Poor Willie, he never slept in a bed that neat in his life. He must feel like he's sealed up in an envelope, ready to get mailed to heaven."

She frowned. "Only . . ." she hesitated, crooking her finger; Harry bent to listen as she whispered.

"Indeed." He nodded judiciously. "An excellent idea, Mrs. Remington. Come along to the nursing desk, and I shall take care of it at once for you."

Blinking, Edwina followed along too, beginning to feel like the third who always makes a crowd. What was Harry up to?

"It's not that I mind some religion," Mrs. Remington was saying, "but it just doesn't fit the picture. That boy doesn't need his dying to look good to him, not now. He needs—"

"Precisely." Harry handed her a prescription

slip. "Take this to the pharmacist, who will give you what's required. In," he added with a conspiratorial smile, "a brown paper bag."

Mrs. Remington nodded smartly. "There, you see? I knew you would have the solution." She turned to Edwina. "That man," she affirmed, "is what I call a doctor."

"Harry, what in the world did you give her?" Edwina asked when the woman had departed satisfied, her head held high and her expression grimly optimistic.

Harry shrugged. "Girlie magazines. Willie loves 'em. Did love them," he amended with a faint frown. "She wants to put up some pictures from those magazines but she's embarrassed to buy them at the drugstore. So I wrote her a prescription for them." He sat behind the desk, pressed the tips of his fingers together. "Can't hurt him now. And besides, she wants to do something."

"And Willie?" Around the desk the evening routine of vital signs and P.M. medications was beginning, clipboards and cardexes waiting in rows on the med carts while nurses drew up syringes full of liquids and dropped tablets and capsules into small plastic cups.

Harry sighed. "Willie had an EEG today, and it was flat. Two more like that and they'll want to take him off the ventilator, let him go. I won't have any say in it, and what I'll tell his mother if it comes to that, I just cannot imagine."

"Oh, Harry, I'm sorry."

He reached for a chart, opened it. "Well, cross

that bridge when we come to it, I suppose.
Thanks for coming up, anyway. I didn't know at
first what she might be getting at, and lately you
never can tell when you might need backup.
Speaking of which . . ."

"Right. I'll call if I do." With Harry at the desk
already stomping out more diseases—as she departed he was shouting into the telephone, demanding that the blood work he had ordered be
drawn now, immediately—it occurred to her that
she did not want to leave the hospital's routine of
specific tasks performed in specific ways, at specific times and places. It no longer included her,
yet it was familiar, predictable, and purposeful,
unlike whatever awaited her in the next few
hours or days.

Also, a remark of Mrs. Remington's troubled
her, although she could not quite put her finger on
why. Doesn't fit the picture, she mused, riding
down in the elevator to the lobby. There, to her
surprise, she found Mona Weissman just hurrying in.

"I drove my father's car into town," said Mona.
"I couldn't stand being in the house any longer,
and besides I might as well drive it. I mean, we
can't very well bury it, can we? And Mother's
asleep, I gave her a pill. It's the only way I could
get the housekeeper to stay."

The girl looked sideways up at Edwina, her face
pinched and white in the streetlights as they
strode along toward Edwina's apartment building. "What are you going to do now?" she asked.

"I'm not sure," replied Edwina slowly. "Did your father ever talk about Vinnie Perillo? He had a small lab just down the hall from your father's—"

"That little creep," Mona said. "No, he didn't talk about him, but I met him once. That was plenty. It was at a party Mrs. Larsen had at her house, actually, for an anniversary of the journal. He wangled an invitation, Perillo did, and he brought along a girl from his lab. She was nice. I don't know what she was doing with him, though. Her name was . . . Carol? Or something like that. Why, what's he got to do with any of this?"

Fumbling a moment with the new lock on the apartment door, Edwina explained about Vinnie's journal piece, and about how bad it had made him look. "I'm wondering if he might have realized that before his father called him, possibly even before the first copies of the issue came out, but too late to stop publication." The door swung open and Maxie strolled into view, looking smug at the yelps of the dog still shut into the bathroom.

"You mean his own father and mine got together and decided to humiliate him?" Mona looked disapproving.

"Well, it was supposed to be for his own good. He couldn't be stopped from making a laughingstock of himself, he was getting worse and worse about it. I gather they thought it might somehow shock him to his senses."

"And maybe he tried to stop its being published, you mean? But how would killing my father accomplish that?''

Edwina sighed. ''I don't know. I don't see what sense it would make.'' She opened the bathroom door and the dog burst joyously out at her, shivering with happiness at having company at last. ''Mona, would you mind taking care of these creatures, please? They'll both need to be fed, and the dog needs a—''

''Walk,'' Mona completed briskly. ''No problem, and no, I will not let anyone nab me while I'm taking the dog out.'' She moved about the rooms, snapping on lamps and surveying everything with her usual crisp, pleasant efficiency.

''Maybe,'' she said, ''Vinnie Perillo just lost his temper.''

Edwina sank into a chair. ''Maybe. But if that's so, then he lost it three times, on three widely separate occasions, and I just can't accept that very readily. I'd rather have a nice sane motive. We've already got one nut case in this situation, and it's simply too much of a coincidence to think we might have two.''

Mona stiffened. ''Excuse me,'' she said in a stony voice quite unlike her usual friendly tone, ''but if by any chance you happen to mean me . . .''

''Oh, for heaven's sake, of course I don't.'' Edwina got up. ''I'm sorry, Mona, that was tactless of me, wasn't it? I was just thinking aloud. Certainly I didn't mean you.''

The girl relaxed, a shy smile replacing her defensive stare. "Oh. All right, then. I guess I am a little sensitive. Sorry."

Snapping the red leather leash to the sheepdog's collar, she went out. Edwina heard her chatting pleasantly to the animal as they moved away down the hall, and then the elevator doors closed on the sound of them.

He's nearer than you think, Craig Fellowes had said about Perillo. But somehow she did not care to put her faith in that. He'd cleared out too quickly for a man who meant to come back. Meanwhile, there was that creaking sound behind Fellowes' voice on the telephone; it had been there during the second call as well, and it infuriated her with its familiarity. Where had she heard it? So commonplace and regular in its constant, rusty ratcheting, like . . . Drat. Whatever it was, it would not come.

The apartment seemed to stretch out, empty and silent. At this hour, McIntyre should be pouring her a glass of wine, perhaps while inventing something delicious in the kitchen. Edwina wandered there herself, poured some wine and took a sip, dumped the rest down the sink and resisted smashing the glass.

Something didn't make sense, that was all. Perhaps Vinnie killed Bennett Weissman in a rage and somehow covered it up. He was clever enough for that. But why Marcia Larsen and the lab technician? Why kill them?

Craig Fellowes was the only one in the whole horrid business whom she felt she understood even dimly. It was a mad game he was playing, but it was a game with rules. With only his voice to go on she felt somehow certain he would keep to those rules, rigidly and with the stubborness of a small, angry child.

So: find Vinnie. Deliver him, alerting the police only at the last moment when it would be too late for them to do anything but go along with the plan, and take her lumps for it afterward.

Unless of course she could find Fellowes first and he turned out to be vulnerable somehow. If she found him in a place from which he could be taken without endangering McIntyre, she would cheat in spades, call the police herself, tell them all she knew angrily and at once. But this seemed even less likely than locating Vinnie. To find Craig Fellowes she would need to know a great deal more than that he was angry, clever, and insane. Only, she didn't know much more, and wasn't at all sure how to go about finding out.

The door slammed, and Maxie trotted to welcome Mona and the dog, both of whom seemed refreshed by their outing. Edwina listened distantly to Mona's chatter, most of which concerned her problems with her mother and how she planned to handle them. Still in her mind's ear the creaking sound squeaked back and forth, maddening and unenlightening. The telephone did not ring, and the moments marched on as Edwina ate without tasting the food Mona placed before her, drank the drink she mixed for her, and regarded twice a minute the chair in which McIntyre ought to have been sitting.

". . . tubes," said Mona.

Edwina blinked. "What? I'm sorry. What was that you were saying?"

Mona looked patiently at her. "I said my mother took pills, and they had to get them out of her with tubes. But never mind, you shouldn't have to be hearing about that, I was silly to mention it. It was quite a long time ago."

She rose, began to clear the plates. Edwina got up, too. "No," said Mona, "sit. I'll do it. We have a bargain, you know, I'll live up to my end of it." Racking the dishes into the dishwasher, she proceeded to gather up the trash and ready it for the hallway trash chute. As she came back into the apartment, the telephone rang.

"I'll get it," she said comfortably, and strode to the small cherry desk where the instrument was shrilling, but Edwina beat her to it. I can, she thought, answer my own telephone, whereupon Harry Lemon's voice came through the line.

"I haven't got much time," he said. "Willie's cousins are here making a fuss, as usual. But the reason I'm calling is that I was down in the pathology department a little while ago."

"Yes, Harry," Edwina replied patiently, feeling a little prickle of excitement. Harry almost never phoned anyone except to demand some immediate action on behalf of one of his patients. His call now meant he'd learned something very interesting indeed.

"And," he went on, "I really thought you might like to know that I overheard two pathology residents talking about the blood alcohol levels on Bennett Weissman. I'm not on a speaker phone or anything at your end, am I, Edwina? Good. Well, the thing is, there's only so much booze a person can drink without simply passing out, you know, let alone staying awake enough to drive a car. And we know the blood alcohol level that much drinking produces, don't we? The lab doesn't lie. Which means, if I am not mistaken—"

"It means," she said, "he couldn't have."

"Right. He was too drunk to drive *or* shoot himself. That's what the boys from pathology were discussing, you see. And it was a serious lapse on the medical examiner's part, and I gather it's a question that's going to be raised on pathology grand rounds, and after that with the M.E.'s office, which among other things is probably going to reopen the Weissman case. Sorry, I must run," finished Harry abruptly, and hung up.

Slowly, Edwina put the telephone down. In the kitchen, Mona hummed a little tune as she wiped the countertops, while Maxie twined about her ankles and the sheepdog sat panting comfortably.

"Mona, were you telling me that your mother had attempted to commit suicide, that she'd taken pills of some sort and had her stomach pumped?"

"Uh-huh." The girl rinsed the dishcloth, wrung it out, and hung it on the towel rack to dry. The kitchen gleamed spotlessly and the animals' water had been freshened, Maxie's bowl of kibble dumped and washed and its contents replaced. "If she hadn't had her stomach emptied, they told us, she probably would have died."

She shuddered. "It was horrible, though, all the

tubes and things. If people realized how repulsive it is, they'd never try it. Not that way, anyway. Why, though? Do they think my father took some? Is that what the phone call just now was about?''

"No," Edwina replied. "I was wondering, is all. Now, you've been very helpful, Mona, but I think I'll try to get some sleep. There's nothing left to do here tonight, and since you've got a car you might as well just go on—''

Mona's look turned to one of dismay. "Oh, please don't make me. I'd . . . really, I'd much rather stay here. The housekeeper is with Mother, she'll be all right."

And, Edwina thought, you've found a place where people don't rage about screaming at you, making demands on you in one breath and accusing you of things in the next. It must, she realized, be like paradise to the girl.

"All right," she relented. "You can stay in the spare room. But just for one night, Mona, don't try working it into any more. I'm not in the market for live-in help, no matter what happens."

Her throat closed briefly on these final words; only knowing that she now had a plan and was about to act on it restrained her voice from trembling.

Fear, she reminded herself, is just heaven's way of telling you to get it over with.

"Go on, now," she told Mona gently, "take some books, and there's a television in there. You can borrow a nightdress from me, and a new toothbrush from the cabinet if you need one. But

I want privacy this evening, so amuse yourself, all right?"

"Yes, ma'am," the girl murmured with a grin, and Edwina held back an exasperated sigh; Mona was by turns so pitiful and so charming, and was such a truly useful little helper, that it really was too bad to have to lie to her.

"What I can't figure out," said Frank Malley, "is whether you're the smartest or the dumbest woman I ever met."

"Would you settle for both?" Edwina eyed the tough old cop over a glass of beer, in the pizza joint where his wife had said he could probably be found. The place was a stucco storefront with a counter and a row of red leather booths tucked into the low-rent end of a shopping center. When she arrived Malley was in the back booth, eating a medium pie with double mozzarella.

"I mean," she elaborated, "I used to think I was smart, and I can't quite face the fact that I really must be pretty dumb if all I can think of is to call you. But," she took a sip of beer, "it is all I can think of, and besides I did promise to. So I'm hoping things will average out somehow."

It was just past midnight; having programmed her telephone to forward calls to the cellular phone and checked to see that Mona was asleep— the soft, regular sound of her breathing had confirmed this—Edwina had crept silently out of the apartment to the car, telephoning Malley as she drove.

Now Malley chomped his way through another

slice of the pizza, looking as if he wished he were not hearing any of this.

"Because you're his friend," she insisted stubbornly, knowing that if he would not help she was sunk. "And you know the kind of thing that happens when SWAT teams start swatting and various people start grandstanding. They're good cops and they mean well, but—"

"But he's got a weapon, too, this nut case. Better just to defuse the whole thing, you're thinking. What about me, though, I'm a year from retirement? I could lose my pension, everything."

Malley shook his close-clipped silver head. "Nah, I don't want it. I'd love to get the jump on those New Haven jokers, always think they're so much hotter'n us suburban cops. But it ain't worth my badge, and that's what it could cost me, things go wrong. My wife'd have my tail in the wringer then for sure."

He pushed his beer away, slid out of the booth. "Besides, you don't know where this guy is— where *either* of them is, Fellowes *or* Perillo—and both of 'em are bad guys. You're gonna bring 'em together for what, a little meet? Right, and I'm Herbert Hoover."

Edwina watched the bubbles in the beer dissolve. "Okay. I just thought he helped you out one time, that's all. But never mind, I guess you're right. I'll go downtown, it's what I should have done in the first place."

Malley looked long suffering. "Christ, you want

to bust my stones about that, now? I never should have told you."

She looked up. "No, really, it's okay. I just had an idea and I didn't want to try it out alone. But never mind, I'll just think up a story for the cops about why I didn't tell them before what I'm going to tell them now, that's all."

She swallowed some of the beer. It was warm and flat and it tasted horrendous. "And then they'll arrest me for obstructing and concealing and who knows what all. You mind if I finish this pizza? Might be the last decent food I'll eat for a while."

She reached for the remaining slice; Malley put his hand out and stopped her.

"Girlie, I'm gonna ask some questions and you better give me some straight answers. First, what makes you think this maniac'll stick to his word? I mean, he's a nut case, ain't he? Who knows what a guy like that might do?"

She picked up the slice of pizza, bit into it, and chewed as she organized her thoughts. Decent was being generous. The stuff was soggy, gluey, and bland, but it gave her time to think.

"Crazy people," she said slowly when she had washed down the horrid morsel, "aren't crazy the way most people believe. They don't do their crazy things at random. They do them according to ideas or feelings quite rigidly arranged within themselves—on account of a chemical imbalance sometimes, and sometimes not."

Malley listened skeptically, but with interest.

"Either way, the rigidness of it all is the trouble," she went on. "It means they can't grow or change. They can't alter their worldview to fit new information. Instead, they'll change the information so that it fits, even by perceiving it wrongly if they're forced to."

Malley nodded slowly. "Who cares about the worldview," he gave the words a cynical twist, "of a guy who's killed a bunch of women?"

Edwina stifled impatience. "Look, he thinks he's required to punish people. He's only holding Martin to get us to let him go on punishing them. He doesn't even want Martin; he wants Perillo, to punish *him*."

"Great," Malley growled, "but even if you're right, how you gonna get this Perillo guy to go along with your goofball plan? He's gonna walk up to this maniac on his own steam, like outta the goodness of his heart, hey? I mean, he's already offed half the medical center. He's gonna care about one cop?"

Gently she angled her head at his service revolver, hanging in the big leather holster at his hip. "First we find Fellowes," she replied, "and then we persuade Perillo to go along with us."

Malley gave a grudging chuckle. "You're nuts yourself, you know that?"

Edwina ate more pizza. The stuff kind of grew on you after a few bites, like some virulent, clingingly greasy subspecies of garlic-and-oregano-flavored mold.

"Look, I told you I can't do it alone. Especially without a weapon, and I do not have one. Although . . ."

"Although what?"

"Well, if you did help me and things went wrong, you could say I took your weapon away and forced you to go along with me."

"Yeah, right," Malley answered incredulously, "and then we say you jump tall buildings in a single bound and stop speeding locomotives by standin' on the railroad tracks."

He shook his head in rejection. "No way no civilian gets my weapon off of me, and especially not any lady civilians. And you got zero chance of findin' Perillo anyway, so . . ."

"I didn't say I had to find Perillo," she replied, chewing.

Malley turned, his small blue eyes alert.

"Craig Fellowes says Perillo is going to find me." She wiped her lips with a flimsy paper napkin, took another to scrub pizza grease from her hands, and got up.

"Maybe you'd want credit for the collar? You might as well. There sure won't be anyone else there to take it."

Which was ridiculous, absolutely ridiculous. Vinnie Perillo was no more going to find her than Willie Remington's paint-by-numbers Jesus was going to float down tomorrow morning on a cloud, with Craig Fellowes at his right hand and McIntyre at his left.

She would have to find Perillo and Fellowes, too, and she was not about to try doing that without some serious backup, of which Malley at present was the only example available. She hoped he would forgive her later for lying through her teeth to him—or, even better, that he would never have to know she had done so.

"The thing is, I've got a good idea how to figure out where Craig Fellowes is, but never mind. You're right, it's just too crazy. We'll have to let the higher-ups take care of McIntyre."

She looked at the long scar creasing Malley's face from his jawline to the bony prominence of his eyebrow.

"Like they took care of you." She turned away.

"Damn," groused Malley, striding past the jukebox, slapping a twenty on the counter, straight-arming the door. "You're lucky there's no other cops in here, all I got to say to you, no one'll ever get the chance to throw this one in my face. You are lucky, McIntyre's lucky, I'm the only one in this damn thing ain't so . . ."

Lucky. "Right," said Edwina, "let's get in the car."

TEN

Sometimes all you could do was shake the tree and hope what fell out didn't grab you by the throat. Thinking this, Edwina pulled the little Fiat out onto Route 10 and headed back toward New Haven.

After retrieving his kit bag from the squad car parked in the lot behind the pizza joint, Malley had gotten into the front seat agreeably enough— agreeably, at any rate, for Malley. "No way I'm gonna get caught in the town's unit on this fool's run," he'd explained, tossing his blue canvas satchel into the back.

"If it is a fool's run," which it was, but she hoped she would figure a way to change that before he found it out, "why are you helping me?"

Malley glanced out the Fiat's open window, locating the right-side mirror and adjusting it casually. "Ain't. But I see I can't talk you out of it, so I'm just ridin' along, keep you from gettin' killed doin' what you're gonna do anyway."

He adjusted the mirror again. "Whatever that is," he added, "which I hope you are gonna enlighten me, you get around to it."

"Look, I told you, all I have to do is—"

"Yeah," said Malley, his gravelly voice unfooled. "You got no more idea how to find Craig Fellowes than I got, how to jump off a ten-story building and fly."

He glanced in the mirror once more. "You bring a friend?"

She frowned into the rearview. Another car, five lengths back or so, kept casual pace. "No. How long has it been there?"

"Since the lot. Prob'ly nothing. Hell, it ain't against the law to drive into town, late."

She slowed; the car behind them dropped back another length as if to avoid tailgating.

"Or maybe it's your buddy Perillo," Malley said, but as he spoke the car turned off onto a side street, in an area of short residential blocks.

They drove in silence through Centerville and Whitneyville, with their small shops, banks, and churches, then past the Eli Whitney barns and onto Whitney Avenue, stopping occasionally at a light. Only a few lamps still burned behind drawn curtains in the windows of the comfortable-looking houses. The night air was soft, and an occasional pair of late night strollers or dog walkers moved along the tree-shaded sidewalks.

"It was a dog like that one," Malley said suddenly. "The time when McIntyre helped me out, I mean."

He pointed to a shepherd pacing at its master's

heel. "But bigger, dogs at the academy were bred for size. For training, we hadda confront 'em without a weapon, see, 'cause the bad guys got dogs, too, and sometimes they'll set 'em on you."

He paused, remembering. "So you get all padded up, your arms and all, and the trainer, he makes a hand signal, sets the dog on you."

"That sounds scary." She turned onto Chapel Street, heading for Edgewood Park, past the British Art Museum and the Yale Repertory Theatre, leaving the newly refurbished buildings of upper Chapel for the red-light district with its pimps and prostitutes scurrying in the gloom, its broken wine bottles glinting from the gutters.

Malley made a noise. "Freakin' terrifying, is what it is. So I happened to be first in line. The dog makes his run at me, an' somethin' goes wrong. And the trainer, he can't get him off me. Come to find out, the dog hadda ear infection, the thing was all whacked out of shape. My luck, get a hurtin' dog."

Edwina slowed, peering at the street signs. Snooping in Marcia Larsen's house, she'd found a body; in Vinnie Perillo's, a potential helper in the person of Smith, but not much more. Maybe the third time would be the charm.

A few cars moved on these streets, mostly older models with dents and rust, the mufflers hanging and the suspensions shot. She found the corner she wanted, turned. "So then what happened?"

Malley took in their whereabouts without comment, as if he had somehow been expecting this.

"Then," he said, "I'm on the ground, dog's on top of me, got his teeth sunk in right here."

He tapped the place where the long thin scar began. "Whole place is goin' nuts, the trainer's yellin' and the dog—when he lets go where he's clamped on—next place he's gonna go for is my throat. Because this dog, see, he is not with the freakin' program no more."

She pulled the car to the curb. Between an extinct dry cleaning shop and a vacant lot littered with trash stood an old brick rowhouse tenement with a sagging front porch, smashed windows in the upper stories, boarded-over lower windows, and a brand new front door, its new lock winking in the light from the block's only working street lamp.

Malley eyed the tenement. "Which is when your old man pulls his service revolver," he went on, "he's standin,' oh, a good thirty, forty yards away, he fires off a number and the freakin' dog, he lets go my face. 'Course," he added, "he wasn't an old man then, McIntyre. He was maybe twenny-two, twenny-four years old. I was older, never mind how much, taking courses 'cause I was buckin' for promotion."

She put the car in neutral and turned. "You mean Martin fired his weapon and scared the dog? But I thought you said—"

"No, I mean he fired his weapon and killed the dog. Helluva shot, too. So that's why I come along, okay? You wanna know more, you can consult the academy yearbook, there, all right? They got all the gory details immemorialized in print.

Now, you bring me here, this slum, for a reason? Or are we just hittin' the high spots?''

Down the block a car turned slowly from a side street, and a woman in a black spandex jumpsuit and platform heels hurried out to meet it. When the car pulled away another replaced it, idling with its headlights off.

"Christ," Malley commented, "I was a New Haven cop, I could sit here, make busts all night. You plannin' answering my question, or what?''

"Well, I could answer it. But I'm worried that if I do answer it, you might leave."

Malley snorted. "Yeah, and then I'll walk home. Come on, girlie, spill your guts. I'm an old cop, remember? You can't tell me anything I ain't heard somethin' a whole lot stupider somewhere else.''

She took a deep breath. "Okay. The thing is, I don't know where Perillo is, and I also don't know where Fellowes is. But I need Fellowes *first*. I need to know where Fellowes is *before* he calls me again, so I can alert the police and probably hospital security *before* I bring Perillo to him. So, I'm *looking* for him first."

"Perillo," Malley said skeptically, "is just gonna let you hand him over so this loony tunes can do what he wants to him?''

"And," she went on, ignoring this—for one thing, she had absolutely no answer to it; with luck, Smith might be able to help locate and persuade Vinnie but there was as yet no guarantee of that—"to find people it is *sometimes* helpful to look at their stuff. You know, their rooms, their belongings, their—"

"Clues," Malley said in disgust. "Help me, Lord, she wants to go in and look for clues, snuffle around amongst the rats and the boards with the rusty nails in 'em, there."

"Look, this is where they got Fellowes. His stuff is still down there, the evidence people haven't finished the sketches or the photographs yet. If I get a look, I might just get an idea how he's thinking, how he's making his decisions. Such as, his decision about where to be right now."

"Yeah," he said, "*if* he's thinking, which is doubtful."

But he got out of the car, pulled his bag from the back seat, and turned to regard the crumbling tenement balefully. By the time Edwina caught up with him he was on the porch, fiddling the new front door lock with what she recognized as one of her own nutpicks.

"Right about now the prowl car pulls up, I'm dead meat," he grumbled, but then the tumblers fell and the door swung open on a wreck of an entrance hall.

Malley pulled a flashlight from his bag, stepped inside. "You coming, or what?"

A car cruised slowly down the street, headlights strobing the landscape of devastation and neglect. Edwina stepped inside, grateful for the oval path of light shed by Malley's flashlight.

At least she was grateful until a small creature skittered through the light and vanished, squeaking, into the stinking gloom. She gasped and hurried after Malley, who was moving deeper into the hall.

"Not quite so tough as you like to make out, hey?" Malley chuckled. "Hey, don't worry, I hate 'em myself. Be spiders too, and prob'ly roaches an' what all. You scream, though, I'm gonna bonk you one with this flash. Cellar door," he went on, "oughta be somewheres around . . . yeah, here." He ducked into an alcove under the staircase, grasped a tarnished knob and pulled.

To Edwina's surprise, the door swung open without sound, and then she realized: Fellowes had oiled it so that no one would hear when he went in and out. She moved toward the pitch-black opening; Malley put an arm out to stop her.

"Hey," he said softly, cocking his head toward the cellar door, from which a cool dank smell drifted.

With the smell came voices. Her eye caught a flickering glimmer from somewhere below, as Malley's hand moved to his side and she heard the sound of his holster strap unsnapping.

"If *we* could pick the lock," she began, "some-one else could have—"

He shook his head. "Nope. That thing was cherry. Other way in, other way out too, I bet. Kids, maybe."

The voices rose more clearly. They were not the voices of children, but of men. The high, desperate one belonged to Vinnie Perillo; the lower one belonged to Vinnie's keeper, Smith.

She grinned at Malley in the gloom. "One

down, one to go," she said. The banister felt slick and greasy, but the steps were clear and intact and no creak gave away her tread. As she descended the glimmer brightened, revealing an ancient boiler, some washtubs, a jumble of junky abandoned furniture.

At the landing she turned, expecting to see Malley still a few steps back. But he was right behind her.

Malley's service revolver was gripped securely in his pudgy right hand, and the expression on his face was all business. Edwina stepped aside to let him pass. Then his left hand moved in a summoning gesture; stepping carefully on the damp, earthen-smelling floor, she followed him among piled crates, between heaps of ancient, sodden rags, and under rusting pipes.

At last the pale faces of Smith and Perillo showed, arguing intently in the corner of the cellar, lit by a flickering candle.

". . . I can't," said Perillo, "they already think I—"

"You must," said Smith, "if you run off now, they'll surely think you . . ."

The corner of the cellar was arranged like a little campsite, with a few battered pans, a plastic cup and some jugs of bottled water, a bedroll, and a row of books. Fellowes' things, Edwina realized, peering about. Two sticks of wood nailed roughly into a cross hung from the wall, fixed there with long strips of electrician's tape, beside a picture of Jesus crudely snipped from some magazine.

Other symbols, less scrutable, had been daubed on the walls: blue handprints and primary-colored runes, faces with third eyes thumbprinted into their foreheads, a kaleidoscope of bright superstition. The air here seemed all at once chill, like the draft from an open freezer.

The books, Edwina saw, were children's books, and the things dangling from the pipes to one side of the camp area were chains, wired together with coat hangers. Four of them hung together, their lower ends fastened to a rectangle of scrap wood to form a seat.

Like a child's swing, Edwina thought as Malley stepped from the shadows into the light, startling Smith and Perillo into sudden silence. Like . . . a child. An angry, dangerous child.

"Don't you move a goddamned inch," Malley said. "I'm a cop."

"I don't . . ." began Perillo, shrinking back at the sight of the gun.

"See here," offered Smith, beginning to rise, dusting his hands against his trousers.

"Sit," Malley snapped. "Both of you sit right down on the floor there and keep your hands where I can see 'em."

He gestured Edwina forward, then aimed the flashlight at the ceiling to illuminate Fellowes' entire den in its reflected glow. She wished he hadn't; the rafters were daubed with the same weird handprints and symbols as the walls, figures mocking and capering and the shadows moving there.

"Vinnie," she began, "I want you to come with me. If you'll help me, I'm certain I can help you."

His frightened eyes regarded her. "How did you find me? This was the *last* place I thought anyone would—"

"The last place anyone would look is the first place *to* look," she told him, trying to ignore the cellar's clammy chill. Never mind, either, that she had found Vinnie only while searching for some clue to Fellowes' whereabouts. He had to believe she was in control or he would never go along with her.

"I want," she began again. As she did so Smith's head came up alertly, at a soft, scuffing sound as of someone moving across the cellar through the darkness beyond Malley's flash. For a moment the silence was like a held breath. Then came a crash of falling crates, a breathless scream, and the scrambling sounds of someone struggling from beneath something.

Spying his chance Vinnie lurched up, whereupon Smith socked him neatly on the jaw and he sat down again.

"Didn't know I could still do that," Smith remarked, rubbing his knuckles and looking pleased. "Don't be an idiot, please, Vincent, my patience with you is wearing rather thin at this point."

"Gah," said Vinnie, blinking and exploring the corner of his jaw with his fingers, which was when Edwina noticed that Malley was not there anymore. Instants later he emerged from the shadows with a small wriggling figure in his grip.

"Just what I needed," he grumbled, "another goofball to go with the *other* goofballs."

Biting her lip, Mona Weissman gazed about, found Edwina and fixed her with a look of fright. "Please," she appealed, "don't be mad at me."

Staggering as Malley released her, Mona clutched the chains from which Craig Fellowes' makeshift swing hung, sank onto its seat, and lowered her head in contrition.

"I just wanted to know what you were doing," she said. "I only pretended to be asleep when I heard you getting ready to go out and then I followed you. I just wanted to know what you were finding out about my father."

The three men stared at her: Malley in disgust and Smith and Perillo in a sort of stunned bemusement, with Vinnie glancing into the cellar's shadows at intervals as if wondering what ungodly new surprise might step forth next.

Mona kicked morosely at the floor; in response, the swing moved back and forth, its rusting chains emitting a rhythmic, rasping creak.

"I shut the dog in the bathroom again," Mona said, "and I locked up the apartment with the spare keys Mr. Brandt gave you, and then I followed you, mostly along the side streets so you wouldn't get scared and think I was somebody else, somebody who might—"

But Edwina was not listening to her words. "Do that again," she said.

"What?" Mona frowned, then kicked again at

the concrete. The swing creaked back and forth once more. A toy, Edwina realized, a child. Toys and children.

"Keep doing it," she said, searching her memory for sight and sound together, finding them at last: children on swings, rising and falling, the swings on rusty chains because they were outdoors, exposed to weather. Outdoors, yet within reach of a telephone in Chelsea Memorial Hospital. . . .

And then it came to her: where Craig Fellowes was.

For all his refusal to admit that he had done anything wrong at all, much less commit three murders, Vinnie Perillo proved surprisingly easy to convince. A few hours crouched alone and uncomfortable in Craig Fellowes' basement hideout had taken most of the starch out of him. Finally he had crept out, making his way through the slum streets until he found a working pay phone, and called Smith to ask him for his help.

Now he slumped defeatedly at the dining room table in Edwina's apartment, alternately protesting his innocence and questioning every detail of Edwina's plan.

"Vincent," said Smith, "we won't really be handing you over to this killer person, only making it look that way so he will release this lady's husband. She's arranged it with the police, you see. And afterwards, she will help you—with the authorities, and with your father."

The arrangement had in fact taken some doing.

After depositing Smith and Perillo at her place with Malley to watch over them—and over Mona, whom Edwina planned to scold later—Edwina had phoned Dick Talbot and Mike Rosewater, met them in the hospital conference room, and given them an edited version of recent events. Even so, only the combined failure of the police department and hospital security to locate Fellowes on their own made them listen to her.

"Look," she had told them, "Fellowes is going to call again. When he does, if I don't go where he says and do what he says, he's entirely capable of killing Martin. For, as he calls it, punishment."

The two men looked at one another, unable to refute this.

"And," she went on, "Vinnie Perillo will be in your custody, effectively, the whole time. It's not as if you could lose him. Right now, we're pretty much at Fellowes' mercy. Let's at least try to change that, put him at ours."

"A setup," Talbot mused unwillingly. "We get ourselves in place first, bring in a couple of shooters, wait until McIntyre's out of the line of fire. Perillo too, we hope. And then—"

Edwina frowned. That was not precisely the way she was planning it. If it did go that way, Craig Fellowes would be about as defenseless as a duck in a shooting gallery, and something felt wrong about that no matter how despicable his crimes.

Rosewater caught her look, understood it. "Edwina, his victims were defenseless too, all right?

And we've got patients in this hospital, staff, visitors . . . we've got to get him."

Talbot got up, his decision made. "The start of it'll go your way, *if* we ever get that far."

It was her turn to understand: the rest went by the book, or no deal. And no cheating—not about their getting Fellowes however they wanted to. Dick Talbot was not a person you wanted to cross up, not and ever show your face anywhere in his vicinity again.

"Perillo's only said he knows he'll be charged," Talbot went on, "and nobody's agreeing to give him any special treatment from our end. So I doubt the DA's going to kick. His defense might later, though. He understand that?"

She shook her head. "I'm not his lawyer. But it's not self-incriminating to agree to help the police. He can say he thought it was his civic duty, for all I care."

Talbot eyed her levelly. "You're getting to be a hard woman, Edwina." His voice was tinged with respect, but with caution, too. "Why do I get the feeling you're not telling me everything?"

But before she was forced to answer he went on. "And how do I know where to tell the guys to set up, if Fellowes doesn't call until right before it all happens?"

"Worst case," she replied. "I can try to stall him, give you time to get your people on the scene." But if she told them too soon, they might set it up without her, and that must not be allowed to happen.

Fellowes could see the street from where he

was. Any upset, any hint of a betrayal, and he could kill Martin McIntyre in an instant. So she would have to make sure McIntyre was out first, and Perillo, too, once he had done his part—yet another thing about which she had not been entirely truthful, not to Talbot or Rosewater, or to Vinnie himself. At least, Fellowes could see the street if he was where she *thought* he was—if that, like so much else, had not merely been a trick. Now in the apartment as the minutes ticked by her anxiety grew, until the first faint gray showed in the night sky. It was four-thirty; true dawn would be in half an hour or so.

Abruptly she got up. "I'll be back shortly. Just want to check something."

From the kitchen where she bustled about making coffee and fixing more sandwiches, Mona stared. Smith and Perillo sat up, too; only Malley's expression did not change: boredom mingled with a patience borne of long experience. She dropped the cellular phone into her carryall.

"Call me if anything happens," she said.

"But you can't—" Mona began. Edwina closed the apartment door firmly on the girl's voice, took the elevator down, and strode along York Street toward Chelsea Memorial. Delivery trucks were moving in the predawn gloom on the asphalt patch behind the shopping plaza as the black sky faded faster to gray and the first few cars began passing in the streets.

At the hospital Edwina was admitted by a lobby guard to whom her face was familiar. Score one for me, she thought, hoping it was an omen.

Climbing the service stairs she met no one; on the fifth floor she passed through a waiting area, deserted except for an orderly sound asleep on a couch. A scrub-suited intern scurried past her, too intent on his errand even to notice her. At the far end of the hall, a stunned-looking family huddled outside the double doors of the intensive care unit, deaf and blind to all but news of some patient within. From the waiting area she entered an office corridor where buzzing overhead fluorescents were the only sound. A door led into the older part of the hospital where pediatric, general medicine, and surgery wards had once been located.

Here the walls were institutional green, the floors brightly polished linoleum tiles, and the silence an echoing, long-unbroken presence. The long wards extending off the corridor were empty, the doors of the patient rooms padlocked, and the nursing stations stripped bare. She remembered when they had been busy and full, in the days when, as a student nurse, she had taken her training here.

Recalling also the shuddering, clanking progress of the ancient elevators, she chose another stairwell, this one with solid oaken banisters and tall windows through which the pale dawn sky was now brightening to hazy blue. Silently she made her way to the top floor, exiting to the former children's ward.

From the nursing station here, she could see onto the makeshift playground one floor down, on the rooftop of the adjacent building. Edwina remembered accompanying the children there, with their casts and wheelchairs, their crutches, and their bulky, inconvenient IV apparatus, all of which had to be gotten down an elevator, along a corridor into that adjacent building, and at last laboriously out onto the rooftop.

In those days, in case of emergencies, a telephone had been installed just inside the rooftop door. While the instrument itself was probably long gone, the wiring would still be there. Fellowes might easily have tapped into it.

Unfortunately, the other thing she remembered was still there, too: the safety wall surrounding the rooftop, about four feet high and built solidly of brick at the same time the playground equipment had been installed. Only the chain link fence that had been atop the wall was gone, salvaged no doubt for some other work when the wards here were abandoned.

Now in the still and bluish gloom of the abandoned nursing station, lit only by the dawn through the thickly dust-grimed windows, Edwina could see the metal swing set, the wreckage of the sandbox, and a wooden mazelike structure that had served as clubhouse, jungle gym, and hideout for the livelier of those long-ago patients.

Then, startlingly, she saw Craig Fellowes himself. She took a quick step back from the window, through which he could not possibly have seen her. And yet some instinct made him turn suspiciously.

He was tall, with wiry dark hair and a long, lantern-jawed face, wearing white slacks and a khaki scrub shirt. In the hubbub of daytime hospital routine, he would likely go unnoticed as long as he did nothing too unusual. He gazed a moment longer at the window, then peered over the wall to the street below. Finally, he strode back out of sight to where the wall around the rooftop shielded him.

Now that it was getting light he would stay out of view. No shooter could draw a bead on him behind that wall. Possibly in darkness . . . but the darkness had gone, and by the time it came again she would know who was crazier: Craig Fellowes or herself.

Cautiously she turned once more to the glass, as the real dawn came and lit the windows of the building opposite. Abruptly she recognized what she was looking at: the rear window of Bennett Weissman's office, with the little electric fan still standing in it. And the windows of Vinnie's lab, opaque at the moment but no doubt clear when the light was right. And that, she realized, was how Craig Fellowes knew. He had been there, on the roof.

Watching all along; witnessing. Vinnie, you poor idiot, she thought as she turned away, you'd better hope he's too crazy to testify against you, assuming he doesn't end up too dead, because I think this guy isn't just claiming to know who killed Weissman and the other two. I think he really does know.

She had made her way to the stairwell and started down it when the phone in her bag went off with a shrill, startling *thweep!* She fumbled for

it with fingers suddenly slick; at once Fellowes'
voice came through the instrument.

"I wanted you to know I've been thinking about
you," he said. "And that I've decided to be merci-
ful."

"What does that mean?" she managed. Had he
seen her after all? But the next voice she heard
was McIntyre's, sounding fine although full of
suppressed fury.

"Hi. Can't say much. I'm okay, though. He
means it about the trade. How are you?"

"I'm fine." Fear and relief warred in her, and
she fought to keep her voice steady while moving
down the stairs as fast as she could. If Fellowes
had indeed glimpsed her, this could be a nasty
trick. "Tell him the trade's on, I've got what he
wants. But I'll need to know—"

Fellowes again. "That's it. No more chat. Hear
this?"

The sharp metallic snap of a hammer on an
empty chamber sounded very clearly through the
phone. McIntyre's weapon, she realized.

"Wait. Listen to me, you know the police will
be watching me."

Which in fact they must not be: If they were,
they would be here right now. Talbot must have
trusted me not to leave him in the dark on anything, she thought with a pang of guilt.

"So they'll know where you are as soon as I
meet you," she rushed, "maybe even before if
they figure out where I'm going—"

If he sees them in the street, let him think they
figured it out; don't let him think I betrayed him.

"—so how are you going to get—"

She bit down on the final word, clamped her lips tightly shut. Off the roof, she'd nearly said, and felt her knees tremble at the slip. But Fellowes didn't seem to notice: high on his triumph, high on being in control. What he thought of as "in control," at any rate.

"How am I going to get away? Oh, please," he said, enjoying himself. "That's too easy. I'm going to fly away." His voice went abruptly cold. "But if anyone tries to stop me," he warned, "I'll be very angry. So wait for my next call, and be ready, and don't screw up. Now that we're such good friends—"

He laughed, a high, hideous sound. "I would hate to have to punish you."

The connection broke. He was only a hundred or so yards away, yet as distant and inaccessible as if he were on the moon.

And she no longer cared if someone shot him: The sound of his laughter and of that hammer on the chamber rang too clearly in her ear. He was playing with her like a child with a toy. A malicious child, with a living toy. Craig Fellowes was a man who had no idea—not about what was real; not about what he could really do. Only about what he could get away with, in his world where he had magic powers and he could fly.

Meanwhile she now felt certain she'd done the right thing. Fellowes was protected by his surroundings, and there was just one entrance onto that roof. Starving him out wouldn't work: he'd only exact punishment against his hostage. From this idea her mind turned in utter nausea as she reached the street.

A frontal assault would likely get McIntyre killed, even if Fellowes died with him. It only took a moment, killing someone. But if the department got frustrated enough, Talbot would have to try it; sooner or later he would be forced to, on orders from above. And they would mean well, try hard. And McIntyre could die.

Meanwhile, though, Fellowes was stuck up there, on that roof. Briskly, she stalked back up York Street. He wouldn't dare risk the elevators, and that left him only two exits: the staircase in the building whose rooftop he now occupied, and the one in the building adjacent, from which she had observed him. But Craig Fellowes wasn't going to get that far. Not if she had anything to say about it. Reaching her apartment building, she stabbed the outer lock with her key and slammed inside.

As she entered the apartment they all looked up: Maxie, the sheepdog, Mona Weissman, Malley, Perillo, and Smith. Ignoring them she yanked a cup from a cabinet, slopped coffee into it, and gulped the liquid down, welcoming its scalding heat.

She would wait, and when Fellowes called again she would do what he said. Only, not *precisely* what he said.

"I don't," said Smith several hours later, "quite see how Mr. Fellowes thinks he can get out of this. Surely he must realize the police will be set up, just waiting for their chance to—"

"He realizes," answered Edwina. "But he's gotten away with everything so far. I think that's just brought him to the point where he believes his own publicity—that he has 'powers,' that he can read minds, and so on."

Which, she added to herself, I sincerely hope he can't. Of course there was one other possibility. Perhaps Fellowes simply wanted to go out in a blaze of glory. Whatever the truth was, they would know soon. Fellowes had called at precisely 9:00 A.M. In just a few moments, she would meet him face to face.

The elevator let out into a twenty-by-twenty-foot concrete block penthouse whose inside walls had long ago been painted mustard yellow. At one time the penthouse had held ventilation equipment, heating and cooling mechanicals for the building atop which it perched like a bunker. Now it was swept bare, so that it resembled a large and extremely bleak prison cell. One battered metal door led out onto the playground roof, another into the stairwell.

"What I want to know," Perillo chimed in plaintively, "is how I'm going to get out of this. *And* how I got into it. I was mad at Weissman, and at my father: They set me up to be humiliated."

"Suckered right into it, too, didn't you?" Malley growled at him. "Must've really ticked you off, bright kid like you."

Perillo hesitated, visibly nettled. Then his

shoulders sagged in defeat. "Yeah. It did. No one likes to be made a fool of. Or," he added simply, "to find out he's made a fool of himself. But I didn't hurt anyone, I swear on my . . . on my . . ."

Appealingly he turned to Smith. "You believe me, don't you?"

"Of course I do, dear boy," Smith replied reassuringly. "And you know the plan, it's all been settled. You'll be out there only long enough to get Mr. Fellowes into plain view. Once that's done we'll begin straightening out this other matter, and—"

"Can it," Malley said, "you can jabber later. Just remember once you do get out there, don't make any stupid moves. The weapons guys across the street might take your head off with them high-powered rifles, there, 'stead of the fruitcake's."

"Right," Talbot said quietly, emerging from the stairwell. "It's all set, ready when you are." Behind him half a dozen men in flak jackets looked grim, checking their weapons and preparing to rush the roof should this become necessary, their radios spitting static from a mobile command center down in the street.

"Just get him out where we can see him," he told Edwina, "and the minute you hear anything, drop. You too," he frowned at Mona, "although why you're in on this at all I just don't—"

"Come on, Dick, I'm going along with your end of the deal, you let me have mine, okay?" She put an arm around Mona's narrow shoulders and forced a smile. "Mona's been my support system all through this, and I really need her now. Hey, everybody needs a little hand-holding once in a while, you know? And Vinnie here is going to be too busy playing hostage substitute to back me up.''

"Right," Talbot said doubtfully, his eyes communicating quite a different message. You'd better know what you're doing, his look said.

She hoped she did. "This is crazy," Vinnie complained as they moved toward the door. "What if he just starts—"

"Vinnie, there's a trauma team waiting one floor down. You're in a hospital, remember? You couldn't pick a better place to get shot. *Which* you're not going to," she added swiftly as he quailed. "Of course, you could still take your chances alone, on the murder charges *and* with your father. Worst case, you could study accounting in prison and take that job he's got for you when you get out. If you get out."

Perillo stopped dead before the metal door. He studied it as he considered, then let out a deep, weary sigh of resignation.

"Let's go," he said.

"Ready, Mona? Just stick with me." Edwina forced optimism into her voice.

Mona Weissman nodded. She had a sort of half-stunned look on her face, as if she could not quite believe she was really doing this and wasn't sure she wanted to, any more than Perillo did.

"Good," Edwina said quickly, "I can't tell you how much it means to me, to have you with me. It's just so helpful, Mona."

Which was about the only even half-truthful thing she'd said in days. Here goes nothing, she thought, stepping past Vinnie and pushing open the door. "Craig? Craig Fellowes?"

She took another step and felt herself yanked forward, nearly stumbling on the roof's pebbled asphalt surface. From the corner of her eye she glimpsed Vinnie and Mona staggering out, too, Craig Fellowes' body moving in a blur as he grabbed them and propelled them away from the door, which slammed heavily shut.

Then he was at her side. "You didn't follow *instructions*," his hot, sour breath gusted into her face. "You'll have to be severely *punished*—"

He spun her around, his fingers gripping cruelly, and in the instant of seeing him up close for the first time she was sure she had miscalculated: This was a mistake. Something was happening to Craig Fellowes, some runaway reaction in the scrambled stuff that was his brain. The pupils of his wild blue eyes expanded and shrank, a twitch jerked steadily at his mouth, and the stink that came off him in waves was of metabolic chaos, wildly mismatched chemicals clashing and jangling in his nervous system.

"Come on, Craig," she tried as he scowled at Perillo, "it's not every day I meet a person as unusual as you. And," she hurried, "as powerful." She took Mona's hand. "I just brought a friend along for a little moral support, that's all."

Something—the fresh air, perhaps—had returned a bit of color to Mona's face. Perillo on the other hand looked as if he might die of fright right here, his skin a yeasty beige and his fingers icy when Edwina reached out to grasp them with her other hand.

Fellowes' answering laugh had no humor in it. Still he did appear placated for the moment. "Let go of them and turn around," he said.

She did. McIntyre huddled in the corner where the brick wall that ran around three sides of the rooftop met the concrete blocks of the penthouse. His hands and ankles were tightly bound with cloth strips. For an instant relief washed over her and then Fellowes was speaking again.

"Now," he said, "what we're going to do, here, is this: You get to take someone with you, and I get to take someone with me. That's fair, isn't it? Even trade. Only, the person I take will have to take the punishment. For," he finished nastily, "the deeds that have been done."

"Listen," Perillo piped up, "you've made a mistake, you—"

"Shut up." There was the smack of a fist striking flesh, then the crunch of Vinnie's shoes as he staggered, trying to keep his feet.

Fellowes' hand seized her arm again, turning her. "See there? At night, it's even clearer."

He'd been here a while, she realized from the stacks of canned goods and other necessities heaped near McIntyre. He had been coming here long before his first capture, perhaps using the roof as a base for supply-gathering forays in the hospital buildings.

And from here she could indeed see into Bennett Weissman's office, straight through his inner room to the doorway of Marcia Larsen's cubicle beyond. Shifting slightly, she scanned Vinnie's lab all the way to where the rat cages had stood.

"It's all right about the police," Fellowes breathed. "I knew you'd have to bring them. You couldn't help it. But they can't hurt me now, you know." He giggled. "Oh ye of little faith."

A bead of sweat trickled down her neck, trickling infernally. "Walk over there," he said, "with your husband. Go on, do it. I'd have shot you already if I meant to." The touch of something small and cold beneath her jaw punctuated this remark.

She swallowed hard. "What about the others?"

No answer. She took a small step. "Craig, look, there's no way out of this, off this roof. Why don't you just come in with me? I'm sure I can get you admitted to a—"

His laugh was horribly unfooled. "Admitted to what? To a dungeon with alligators and a moat? No, Miss Crusoe, I'm not going to be admitted anywhere. Only to the kingdom of heaven. Just keep walking. Do what I say." He shoved her hard and she stumbled forward.

"Hey," McIntyre said as she crouched by him. "Good to see you." He sported a huge purple bruise just above his left eyebrow, and his look was full of worry.

"Good to see *you*," she managed. "I've got to get him out where—"

Mona's scream cut her off, spun her around as Perillo came stumbling at her. Still shielded by the wall, Fellowes backed away with one arm around the girl's throat and the gun pressed firmly to her head.

"Hey," Vinnie began injuredly, "*I* was supposed to be the one who—"

"So," Fellowes crooned to Mona, "what do you think? Can I fly? More to the point, can *you* fly?" He angled his head at the wall, which was topped by a flat concrete cap about eighteen inches wide. "Come on," he urged, "let's try it."

"No," Mona shrieked, "*listen* to me, you've got it all wrong! It was *him*, you practically *said* it was him, you *can't*—"

He yanked her head back hard. "I didn't say anything about him. Come on, little girl, weren't you *listening*? I *said* I could see into those windows. I *saw* what you did, little girl. I *saw* you. So why don't you tell the rest of them all about it, hmm? Confession," he advised her, "is good for the soul."

Mona stopped struggling, her eyes wide with realization.

"He's out there, now," Vinnie said. "Why don't they just shoot him?"

"They're afraid they'll hit her," McIntyre said, "and he knows it. What," he asked Edwina, "is on the other side of that wall?"

She had finished untying his wrists and begun on his ankle bindings. "A ledge about two feet wide all the way around, about three feet down. It's just decorative, I'm not sure what it's made of or if it would hold anyone up. After that, seven stories of air and then the sidewalk."

Fellowes was nearly at the wall, now, still holding Mona close to him. "Oops," he giggled, "here comes the hard part. Have to let go of you a minute, but if you run I'll shoot you dead. You do know that, don't you?"

Mona nodded in terror. He released her, and she fell. Fellowes crouched beside her.

"Now," Vinnie whispered urgently.

"They haven't got a shot," McIntyre said. "He's below the damned brickwork." He looked sideways at the door and began sliding himself carefully toward it.

". . . naughty girl," Fellowes said. "But I'll tell you what: You confess and I'll let you go. How's that? Have we got a deal?"

Shakily, Mona nodded. Her eyes, dark with shock, gazed at Edwina in mute appeal. "A-all right. I-I killed them. I just couldn't stand it anymore," she pleaded, "he was giving her *everything* and the rest would go to my muh-mother. So I t-told him it wasn't fair, and he pruh-promised me he would change it. He showed it to me, he *showed* me he changed it. But then I couldn't f-find—"

"Poor baby," crooned Fellowes, "isn't it awful? Isn't it bad when they don't do what you *tell* them? You should come with me, you know. We'll *show* them." He vaulted easily to the top of the wall as with weak scrabbling motions Mona tried to crawl away from him on the pebbled asphalt.

Fellowes crouched, extending his hand. "Now," Vinnie pleaded, "*now.*"

"Upsy-daisy," said Fellowes genially as the first shot struck him, the rifle's cracking report sounding an instant later. He frowned at his left arm where his blood began streaming, then raised the weapon still clutched in his right hand, leveling it once again at Mona.

"Guess what?" he said. "I lied. I'm not letting you go."

"No," Mona Weissman said, cringing below him with nowhere at all to hide.

The second shot struck Fellowes in the shoulder, spinning him but miraculously still not dropping him. So wired up, Edwina realized, he probably didn't even feel it. A smooth and dreamy look of purposefulness spread on his face.

McIntyre reached the door and thrust his arm through it as if for something the men inside might give to him, his muttered words inaudible over Mona's scream. Fellowes fired, his shot exploding the pebbled asphalt inches from her head, and leveled his weapon at her once more.

But before he could fire again a thunderclap boomed in Edwina's ears; a stain bloomed on Fellowes' shirt. For a final moment he seemed to hang there, outlined against the sky, his weapon fallen and his hands clasped prayerfully together, his eyes open and alert and appearing to be—although of course they could not be—entirely red. His lips continued moving steadily as he went over.

Men swarmed onto the rooftop. McIntyre laid down Talbot's service revolver and sighed. "Idiot," he said to the patch of air where Fellowes had been. "I told you this would happen."

"Wow," said Vinnie, staring at McIntyre. Then

came cries of consternation from the uniformed men peering over the brickwork.

Making her way to where the officers were gathered, Edwina leaned out over the wall, steeling herself for what she must see. Malley was there beside her, and so was Talbot. Smith took charge of Vinnie as more officers began readying an apparatus of ropes and pulleys whose purpose she could not at first gather.

But when she looked, no paramedics had gathered in the street below; no sorry shape lay broken upon the sidewalk. On the narrow ledge three feet down, a patch of bright blood showed where Craig Fellowes' body must have fallen.

Only, it wasn't there now. Craig Fellowes was gone.

ELEVEN

"IT'S simple," Edwina said to the little group of friends and well-wishers gathered in her apartment two days and a world of feelings later. "Mona lied, and she was lucky. Or," she amended, "for a while she was lucky."

"If you want to call that luck," Malley put in gruffly, glowering at her from the sofa.

"Right," she agreed. "If you want to." After a day and a night in the hospital for a checkup, tests, and observation, McIntyre had emerged not much the worse for wear. Now he basked in the presence of friends and in the sunshine streaming into the apartment, glinting on the freshly polished fireplace brass and sparkling in the cut-crystal champagne glasses Edwina had set out on the occasion of his homecoming.

"But whatever you want to call it," she continued, "late one night last week Mona visited her father in his office at the hospital. It was only a few days since he'd told her he'd changed his will, cutting out Marcia Larsen and making Mona a direct beneficiary, as Mona had been demanding. She told me they had discussed it, you see, but discussion in fact was not quite what really had occurred.

"What really happened," she turned to inform the rest of the room, "was that he'd tried to prepare her on the topic of his possible death, but instead of accepting what he said, she'd been driving him crazy—threatening to kill herself and similar nonsense if he wouldn't change his mind about his will. He never even got a chance to tell her he was seriously ill. I suppose it must have hurt him that she cared more for the money than for him, and so he never did tell her. Nor about the contraption he'd hidden for himself in his closet, just in case things got too unbearable."

At this, Vinnie Perillo looked uncomfortable. "Maybe she thought he would just live forever," he ventured. "Some people are like that, you know. They just seem so all-powerful to you, you can't imagine them ever dying. You can't imagine you might not get the chance to . . . to . . . well. You can't imagine them gone," he ended thoughtfully, patting at his awful hairpiece.

"Yes, Vinnie. We'll visit your father in the morning, shall we? You and I will pay a social call. Don't agonize, I'm really quite a dab hand at winning over older men."

Malley snorted in disgust, while Vinnie's answer was a wordless look of worry and hope. The tall old oil portrait of her own father gazed down upon them from above the mantel with what from

Edwina's angle appeared to be indulgence. Vinnie was not a bad son, E.R.'s look seemed to say, only feeling a bit chilled in his father's shadow, which was after all rather long and dark. Then Smith spoke up.

"But Miss Crusoe, precisely *how* did she do it? We understand why: She thought she was going to get the money. Still—clubbed, shot, *and* gassed? It seems a bit . . . well, extreme."

"Actually, it was even a bit more complex than that, and its complexity only made it better—more difficult for anyone else to figure out, you see. What you've got to realize first is that she believed he'd changed his will. He even seems to have shown her a document to prove it—one he destroyed, I suspect, once he'd quieted her on the topic. Or at any rate, he thought he had quieted her."

"The document," said Smith, "she was searching for when Mrs. Larsen caught her at it."

"Precisely. Mona had gone so far as to steal his keys to search his office—looking, I suppose, for things she might hold against him, to make him do what she wanted him to do. The only thing she could use was the fact of his relationship with Mrs. Larsen herself, and she didn't dare do that: It would muddy the waters for her own campaign, you see. She wanted things set up the way *she* wanted them, not for her mother to get *her* meddlesome oar in. Which of course her mother did, but that was later. When Weissman found out about Mona's searches, he had his office lock changed—that was why Mona had to wait until

Mrs. Larsen was at work to look for the new will she was certain must be there.

She turned to McIntyre. "That was another thing, of course: that little medical table lying there unsearched amidst an apparent search for drugs. As it turned out, its drawer held old journal covers; Weissman had a collection of them. Mona didn't search the thing, because she knew what was in it. She simply turned it over to increase the appearance of a mindless intruder's impatience."

Smith frowned. "You still haven't answered my question."

"Yes. The method. She had to hit him to knock him out. I suppose she simply struck him from behind with the paperweight. That was one of the first things I noticed: the absence of a paperweight in his office, all those papers blowing in front of the fan. It didn't seem well organized, and Mrs. Larsen at any rate was a well-organized person. The paperweight, by the way, was found among the rocks by the water at the Weissman house today. Poor Mona neglected to check the tide charts before she tossed it there. One of two scientific things she neglected to make sure of, as it happens."

Edwina paused, thinking of fixing herself a drink, but deciding against it. The mental picture of Mona pouring bourbon down the throat of an unconscious Bennett Weissman, using a length of rubber tubing and a funnel filched from Vinnie's lab, promised to enforce a strict mineral water regimen for the short term and perhaps even permanently.

Observing her guests sipping champagne and nibbling little appetizers, she thought she might gloss over the details on this point. Vinnie, however, prevented her.

"What about Caroline?" he asked sadly from where he slumped in an upholstered chair. He was on his fourth glass of champagne, an indulgence she might have put a stop to had Smith not been sticking so virtuously to coffee and keeping the car keys in his pocket.

"She was a smart woman," Vinnie went on, "but she sure hated me after a while. Called me Dr. Fumblefingers when she thought I couldn't hear, and sometimes when she knew I could. Lab sure went to hell once she was gone, though."

He shot a shamefaced look at Edwina. "Christ, what a bloody idiot I've turned out to be."

"Now, Vinnie, don't be too hard on yourself," she said. "I'm afraid Caroline must have stopped in, on her way to pick up her own things, while Mona was helping herself to a few crucial items that were sitting around in your lab.

"Items," she went on delicately, "which she needed to get the required amount of bourbon into her father, so that it would look as if he'd killed himself in an alcoholic stupor. She'd seen you and Caroline at Mrs. Larsen's house one time. I think she chose the burial spot just to confuse matters, to throw suspicion anywhere but on herself. Suspicion to which Craig Fellowes unwittingly added, with his little rat trick."

Vinnie nodded, unhappily but comprehendingly. "I'll bet Mona dumped her in one of those trash bins on wheels," he said, "wheeled her down and backed her car up to the loading dock by the trash dumpsters. Hey," he turned to Smith, "no security there. Who'd want hospital trash?"

At this, Edwina eyed him with rather more respect, thinking that if he ever cared to give up scientific research she might put him to work in research of another sort, since he apparently had the instinct for it. She smiled at him, and he looked gratified.

"You're quite right. When the police came to investigate her father's death, Mona had another body hidden for the moment in her own cellar. The next day, when she knew Mrs. Larsen would be at work, she completed her plan for disposal of it."

"Cut to the chase, girlie," Malley said.

"Indeed." She eyed him cautiously. There was absolutely no sense in antagonizing him. Having gotten away with all this by the skin of her teeth, she did not need his impromptu dental work, most of which he could exercise simply by talking frankly to his old buddy McIntyre.

She glanced at her husband, a delightful creature himself, but one who most assuredly did not need bringing up to speed on details of her own recent activities. Perhaps she could blind him with more science.

"Mona," she said, "was acquainted with tube-feeding methods, having had the reverse procedure performed on herself quite a number of times in various emergency rooms. Another lie of Mona's: She said it was her mother who'd swallowed pills, but that idea didn't sit right with me from the start. Serina Weissman despises other people, not herself. It was why Mona's father believed she might really do it, you see. And it was another thing that didn't make sense: Mona said that bourbon bottle had been there for years. But when I visited the house, Mrs. Weissman was drinking bourbon. A bigger slip was giving him too much bourbon, but she had to keep him nearly out cold to get the gun into his hand, and fire it that way."

At Edwina's feet, Maxie the black cat continued twining sensuously, emitting noises of mingled politeness and greed. "Come on, boy," said McIntyre, bending to arrange a few bits of chicken liver pâté on a cocktail napkin. "You might as well be in on the party, too."

"Once she'd disabled him with the paperweight in his office—it was late, you remember," Edwina went on, "there weren't many people around at that hour—she simply wheeled him down to the hospital's front door and out to his car. When she got him home, she quite coldly finished the task. The gunshot was to obliterate blunt trauma, the marks left by the impact of the paperweight. Nothing like a gunshot wound to eliminate evidence of a clobbering, and of course the car exhaust was to make it seem even more as if he'd done it all himself, under the influence of the bourbon."

"Lying," Dick Talbot put in quietly, "is a sin."

She looked at him. He seemed unusually thoughtful today, or perhaps only grateful that things had turned out as they had.

Just then Maxie noticed the cocktail napkin, made a dash for it, and stopped short at the sight of the dog heading that way, too. Meowing in dismay, he skidded helplessly across the polished parquet floor toward what he clearly believed was his own impending doom.

"Martin," Edwina began, as Maxie's premonitions on this point seemed certain to be realized.

"Wuff," the dog offered, lowering his head as the cat backpedaled madly and to no effect.

"Umph," Maxie uttered, slamming hard into the larger animal's black, glistening, and apparently still tender nose.

"Yike!" the dog cried, recoiling, and for a long instant the two creatures gazed at one another, Maxie in rigid horror and the dog with a look of goofy, wounded puzzlement.

"Grr," he muttered tentatively, searching his memory banks for *cat*.

A moment passed in which it seemed that Maxie's nine lives were about to be consumed wholesale. Then, with an air of absolute, unbending dignity, the black cat got to his feet. Ignoring his audience, and as if no dog had ever been invented much less introduced into his very own home, he turned to devouring chicken livers.

Faced with a choice between ferocity and food, the dog joined in snuffling up hors d'oeuvres, oblivious to Maxie's dirty look which seemed to say that this sort of thing might be all very well for now, but if the supply of treats ever ran low, certain canines had better watch themselves.

"That still leaves the hat," Vinnie said. "Why'd she make such a point of that missing hat, and how did—"

"We found the hat," Mike Rosewater spoke up from where he had been sitting quietly at the dining room table, sipping a cup of tea. "Turned up in the hospital's lost-and-found. We figure if it never showed, she could keep using it to direct attention away from herself, and if it did the little bit of blood in the hatband would show she'd been right all along, what she was saying—someone did something to him. She figured we'd think she *wouldn't* say that if she'd done it herself."

"Miss Weissman," said Smith, "was adept at fitting happenstance into her plans."

"She was," Malley's voice grated, "a stone liar. Like some other people I could mention."

Edwina glanced apologetically once more to where he sat drinking a beer he had fetched for himself from the refrigerator.

"You knew when she showed up in the cellar," he said. "You knew *before* then, even. And you sure as *hell* knew by the time we got up on that rooftop, there."

"Goodness, I can't imagine what makes you think so," Edwina began innocently, refraining from mentioning that she had not *known*, only suspected.

"Hey," Malley said, holding up one stubby finger. "She spots you at the old man's memorial shindig, right away she's all worried about you maybe bein' there snoopin', see what I mean? So she starts right in on the weepin' an' wailin' routine, gets the sympathy jump on you. Guilty conscience makes her think you're involved. She wants to be sure it's on her side all the way, right? An' the more she tells, the less you suspect.

"Next," another finger stabbed the air, "she's all over you, makin' herself indispensable, she hears all the dirt soon as you hear it. *And* she's got herself all that financial motive, there—that what you call your cooey bone-oh. Money in a trust is still money, you know, an' she was gettin' that sooner or later."

He swallowed some beer. "You may be dumb, girlie, but you ain't stupid. You knew you got her up there, that fruitcake'd be all the persuasion she needed. An' you knew *he* was up there, too, which I do not know how you knew, but if this'd all turned out some different way you wouldn't of seen the last of me, I'll guarantee you that much." He belched softly to punctuate this.

"I hope," said Edwina, contrite but undaunted—it had all turned out all right, after all—"I hope I haven't seen the last of you, anyway."

"Hmph," said Malley, heaving himself up. "You got any actual food around here, something a person who doesn't eat fish eggs or mashed up chicken insides could possibly digest?"

Grinning, McIntyre went to help Malley find the peanut butter and some jelly. Meanwhile Dick Talbot still sat alone on the sofa, content

with his lime and seltzer and with his surroundings, which for once were neither dangerous nor
criminal. His breathing was bothering him again,
she noted by the way his chest moved deliberately, determinedly up and down.

Quietly she sat beside him. "Thanks for everything, Dick. I appreciate it."

He nodded, looking troubled. "Glad it worked
out. Funny thing about that Fellowes guy,
though, I wouldn't have said it was possible."

She blinked. "Dick, all he did was crawl into a
ventilator duct at the far end of that ledge. He
didn't need any supernatural powers to yank a
rusty grate. What's amazing was your getting
over there and finding him so fast, when everyone
else still thought he'd vanished into thin air."

"I guess. Funny what you can do when you
don't think about it. You know, when I got to him
I still thought he might make it."

"It happens. He was all pumped up. Probably
the adrenaline kept his blood pressure from
crashing for a while."

He looked at his glass. "Right. And all the
things he knew about people, tricks he pulled off,
like that fire—hell, anyone can do that stuff, they
prepare right. It's just head games the guy
played, facts he overheard, matches and stuff that
he hid."

"Sounds like you're trying to convince yourself."

Talbot gave himself a mental shake, drained
his glass of seltzer. "Nah. It's just that when I got
to him, he didn't look like a murdering bastard

anymore. He looked like a scared dying kid, just like they always look. And he said . . . ah, hell, what difference does it make what he said?'' He set his glass down with a clink.

She peered at him, her curiosity piqued. "So what did he say?''

Talbot shrugged. "Okay, okay, maybe it'll help if I get it off my chest. He said he had one more miracle in him, and I'd know what it was by this afternoon. 'And now for something completely different,' he said. Those were his exact final words. And then he didn't say anything more. He closed his eyes and died.''

He shook his head angrily. "The stupid crazy, I don't know why I even bother remembering what he said.'' Then he softened, smiling with an effort. "But listen, if any miracles do happen today, you be sure to let me know about them, all right?''

"Deal," she said, patting his hand and smiling back at him; good old Talbot, and Fellowes had been horrible. It was no wonder no one could quite forget him.

The telephone rang and she got up, with Maxie and the sheepdog dancing at her feet.

"Edwina," said Harry Lemon as she lifted the receiver. At his voice, backed by sounds of the nursing desk on his ward at Chelsea Memorial Hospital—the pinging of patients' call-lights on the intercom, the ringing of phones and the droning of the overhead page operator, voices mingling in query, consternation and command—at all these sounds she felt a sudden pang of guilt, the problems of Harry's poor dying patient Willie

Remington and the Remington cousins' dreadful lawsuit having fled her mind completely for the past two days.

"Harry, what's the matter? Did Willie Remington die?"

Across the room Dick Talbot turned, a still and expectant look of listening on his face.

"What's happened?" she insisted. "Have the Remington cousins showed up there, again?"

"Yes," Harry said slowly, "they're here. Mrs. Remington's here, too, because Willie's third EEG this morning was flat. So we were going to take him off the life-support, and let him go."

Talbot moved questioningly to stand beside her and after a moment the others looked up, too: McIntyre and Malley from the kitchen doorway where they stood with peanut butter sandwiches in their hands, Smith and Rosewater with cups halfway to their lips, and Vinnie Perillo from an amiably sozzled haze, as the optimism Smith had been trying to instill in him finally began taking hold.

Vinnie, she saw, had at some point been inspired to remove his awful toupee. Now Maxie had dragged this object to the floor and was batting happily at it, apparently in the belief that it really was the small dead mammal it resembled. The fluff of dark fuzz on Vinnie's head, then, must be . . .

Hair. Real hair—*new* hair—sprouting from his scalp. His discoveries, she realized, his experiments. He smiled shyly at her, clambering to his feet and peering about for the coffeepot, which Smith quickly fetched for him.

"Harry," she demanded, "what *is* it? What's happened?"

". . . *were* going to take him off life-support, but then he—"

At the nursing desk, a chart snapped shut. A cardiac alarm jangled briefly. A wire lab basket clanked down onto the desktop. Someone's beeper went off, and someone's phone rang. Then Harry Lemon's voice came through again, tinged with mystification and wonderment.

"Edwina," he said, "an amazing thing has happened here."